THE
CORPSE ON
THE DIKE

Janwillem
van de Wetering

BALLANTINE BOOKS • NEW YORK

Library of Congress Catalog Card Number: 76-18086

ISBN 0-345-33130-3

First published by Houghton Mifflin Company. Reprinted by permission of Houghton Mifflin Company.

Manufactured in the United States of America

First Ballantine Books Edition: May 1987

for my friend Austin Olney

‖‖‖ | ⫿⫿⫿⫿

THE LATE SUMMER EVENING WAS HOT AND HEAVY. DARK clouds had packed together until they covered the sky and the thick light seemed to distort the scene around the two lone fishermen in their small boat on the river. There had been some wind earlier on but now the water around the flat-bottomed dinghy hardly showed a ripple. The fish must have joined the general stillness of their environment, for Sergeant de Gier's float, standing lonely and defiant, sparkling white against the dark gray of the water, looked as if it were stuck in glue.

"If this is fishing," de Gier said, "it is even more boring than I'd thought it would be."

Adjutant-Detective Grijpstra turned his heavy head and pouted his lips.

"This *is* fishing, isn't it?" de Gier asked.

Grijpstra nodded.

1

"And there *are* fish here?"

Grijpstra nodded again.

De Gier studied his float. It wasn't in the same place. It had moved. But how much had it moved? An inch? Or half an inch? He closed one eye. The float had been in line with the trunk of an old chestnut tree ashore and now it wasn't quite in line anymore, so it had moved. Something had happened, for the first time in more than an hour something had happened. His float had moved.

But he didn't really mind. De Gier, in spite of a reputation for efficiency and go-getting, which he had built up during ten years of crime investigation for the Amsterdam Municipal Police, wasn't a highly motivated man. He had worked out, before he stepped into the dinghy that evening, that they wouldn't spend more than two hours on the water. In order to come to that conclusion he had applied logic. They were there for a purpose: to catch an escaped prisoner. The facts he had been supplied with were simple enough. The prisoner, or rather the ex-prisoner, was supposed to be in one of the twelve little ramshackle houses that were leaning crazily against the dike their boat was now facing. If they could see the houses, the occupants of the houses, including the ex-prisoner, could see them. Whoever would be watching them from the windows of the little houses would think they were fishermen. But fishermen fish by daylight. In another hour it would be dark. It would be funny for fishermen to try to fish in the dark and the ex-prisoner would be a little suspicious. So, de Gier was thinking, if nothing happened out there he and Grijpstra would be rowing back. They would moor the dinghy and go home—Grijpstra to watch TV in his little house on the Lijnbaansgracht in the old city of Amsterdam and he, de Gier, to his small apartment in the suburbs to water the flower boxes on his balcony and to feed Oliver, the Siamese cat who would be rolling on the floor as soon as he heard the key in the lock, expecting to be picked up and fussed over. De Gier was looking forward to going home. He liked his flower boxes; his newly planted dark orange asters were doing well lately. He loved his cat Oliver—even if the poor neurotic animal was somewhat impossible—and he didn't like fishing.

What if I catch something? he was thinking. He could see himself trying to pull the hook out of the mouth of a slimy jumping fish and shuddered. He didn't want to hurt a fish. He shouldn't have allowed Grijpstra to bait his hook. Perhaps a fish was approaching the bait right now, his stupid mouth wide open, ready to swallow the sharp curel steel. A fish ought to be caught with a net, in sparkling transparent cool water, off the shore of an island in the tropics. Palm trees. Nut-brown girls dancing around in short aprons made of banana leaves. Birds of paradise fluttering above the undergrowth. De Gier was smiling to himself.

Grijpstra was also smiling. His line of thought had been similar to de Gier's at first but Grijpstra had dreamed himself into actually catching a fish, a big fish, a pike, a big whopper of a pike. He knew there were pike in the river; he had seen a big stuffed one above the counter of a pub on the dike. He had been told the stuffed corpse was only a year old. Why shouldn't he catch a pike now? First catch the pike, then catch the ex-prisoner, and show the pike to the other detectives? What's wrong with success? He was visualizing the jealous grin of surprise on Adjutant Geurts's face. Geurts was an ardent fisherman himself. Grijpstra always enjoyed annoying Adjutant Geurts.

"The light is going," de Gier whispered. "The colleagues will have to hurry out there or it'll be over for today."

Grijpstra grunted. He suddenly changed his mind. He

didn't want to catch the ex-prisoner anymore. He was enjoying himself on the water. Why did they have to bother the unfortunate man? But the man had to be caught, of course. The man had escaped from jail and had, of his own free will, a will that had been suspended by the authorities and that shouldn't be free, interrupted a stretch of three years which an elderly and well-meaning judge, after much deliberation, had imposed because of a combination of broken regulations—regulations created by the state to protect its citizens against themselves. The man should have stayed in his gray concrete cell in the company of a gray metal bunk and a gray metal table and chair. The man should have been patient. But he hadn't been. He had, while he had lived in the filtered light of his cell where the sun could only reach him through opaque thick reinforced glass panes, thought of a plan. And he had executed his plan.

He had picked his nose with a sharp nail, twisting it as cruelly as de Gier's fishhook might twist itself, any second now, into the soft cold skin of the inside of the mouth of a fish. The nail drew blood and the prisoner caught the blood in his cupped hands and smeared some of it on his shirt, sucking the rest into his mouth. Before filling his mouth he had knocked on his door and shouted for the Eye, the nasty Eye who checked him, through a small slit, every hour. The Eye came and found the prisoner on the floor, blood dribbling down his chin. The Eye reported and came back with other Eyes and they took the prisoner to an ambulance. The prisoner had a friend in the hospital and he escaped that same day.

That was three months ago now. The authorities didn't worry much. The police were informed. Adjutant Grijpstra had been called into the commissaris'* office. He was shown the prisoner's file.

"Small fry," the commissaris said, "very small. Not even dangerous. You know him, don't you? Didn't you and de Gier deal with the case?"

"Yes, sir," Grijpstra said and went on reading the file. "Catch him sometime," the commissaris was saying, "but don't go out of your way. No use looking for him. He'll turn up at one of these addresses. Let the informers know; put a small price on his head. Why did he get three years? He is only a burglar, isn't he?"

"Yes sir," Grijpstra said, "but he keeps on being a burglar, that's his trouble. A bad burglar. And unlucky."

The commissaris sighed. "Tell me, I don't feel like reading the file; it's too thick."

Grijpstra looked up and saw that the commissaris had only read a single piece of typewritten paper, with a photograph attached. The photograph showed the face of a bearded man, rather a pleasant face, a face with a sense of humor.

The commissaris gave the sheet to Grijpstra. The Head Office clerks had mentioned three addresses in Amsterdam, explaining that the first belonged to the elderly sister of the criminal and the other two to friends.

"He came quietly when we arrested him that time," Grijpstra said. "Had been breaking into a shop but the owner happened to arrive that evening and caught him on the job. There was a struggle and the owner fell and hurt his head. It changed the charge. The public prosecutor wasn't in a

*Ranks of the Dutch Municipal Police are constable, constable first class, sergeant, adjutant, inspector, chief inspector, commissaris, chief constable. An adjutant is a noncommissioned officer.

good mood. The prisoner's counsel wasn't very clever. Three years."

The commissaris was shaking his head.

"Well, he'll come quietly again. Don't upset him. Talk to him. You are good at that, Grijpstra. And don't rush. Sometimes we must rush and sometimes we must wait. This time we wait."

Grijpstra sighed. "He has been in jail two years, sir. Let's hope he hasn't become violent."

"Yes," the commissaris said. "Jail!"

"Doesn't improve them much," Grijpstra said.

The commissaris agreed but he didn't pursue the subject. The commissaris was an old man, close to retirement. He had been in jail himself, during the war, when the Gestapo had wanted to learn about the way the Dutch Resistance worked. The commissaris had been a senior officer in the Resistance and he hadn't felt like cooperating with the German investigators. The commissaris had been lodged in the same jail the bad burglar had now managed to escape from but the time had been different. A little blood dribbling down a prisoner's chin hadn't impressed the Germans much during those days. The commissaris remembered how he had eaten a piece of bread that one of his fellow prisoners, blinded by blood which ran into his eyes from a cut just above the eyebrow caused by the wedding ring of an interrogating German police officer, had accidentally dropped into the shitbucket. The commissaris had taken the bread out, wiped it clean, and eaten it. It had been a bad jail. It was, in spite of changed circumstances, still a bad jail. But the state needed jails. The commissaris grunted and rubbed his right leg, which was hurting him more that day than his left. The rheumatic pain lessened somewhat and didn't bite as deeply into the bone as it had before. He went on rubbing his leg. He couldn't remove the pain and he couldn't do away with jails.

Grijpstra looked up from the file. "It says here, sir, that the man is close to his sister. Used to live with her. She never married and the man is a widower. So he'll probably look her up. The address is on the dike, do you know the dike, sir?" Grijpstra had gone to the large map of Amsterdam on the commissaris' wall. His thick forefinger traced a rapid course from Police Headquarters to the north, crossing the IJ River and veering off toward the left.

"There," he said, "Landsburger dike."

The commissaris followed Grijpstra's finger and thought. "Yes," he said after a while, "there is a wharf over there, a small wharf. I was called out there once, years ago now, because a laborer had broken his neck falling down a scaffolding. The doctor thought that he might have been pushed, and he very likely was but we couldn't prove it."

"There are some small old houses there," Grijpstra said, "full of funny people. Asocials they are called nowadays. Unemployed. Drunks. Old age pensioners. Half-wits. Small-time criminals. I have been there often, thefts mostly and drunken fistfights when they've had trouble dividing the loot. The man's sister will be living in one of those houses. There was a council plan once to clear the dike and widen it and build blocks of apartments but the houses are old, three hundred years old maybe, and have been placed on the list of monuments. Evenutally they will be restored."

The commissaris was behind his desk again, flipping the pages of a notebook. "We have an informer on the dike," he said.

"I know, sir. He is called the Mouse."

"Do you know him?" the commissaris asked.

Grijpstra pulled a face.

"You don't like him?"

"Who likes an informer?" Grijpstra asked the ceiling of the commissaris' office.

"But you pulled a *very* nasty face," the commissaris said pleasantly.

"He is a nasty man, sir. Squeaky nasty little man. Too small to be called a rat. He gave me a tip last year, turned in his own friend—man he had been playing billiards with for years—and on a very small charge too. But the charge stuck."

"Cheer up, Grijpstra," the commissaris said, "cheer up. We have jails and we have informers. And we have criminals. And we are policemen. And it is raining. Cheer up."

"Sir," Grijpstra said.

Grijpstra shifted his weight and the dinghy moved.

"Easy," de Gier whispered, "sit still. This is a small boat. If you tip it over we'll be in the drink and we'll drown. And if we don't drown we'll look silly. And we'll be wet. Easy!"

"You are a sportsman, aren't you?" Grijpstra asked.

"Not here. This water is bound to be very dirty."

Grijpstra sighed. He started thinking about the ex-prisoner again. He'll be having tea with his sister now, Grijpstra thought. He only came for the day but the Mouse saw him all right and he spent a quarter of a guilder on a telephone call. It'll be on his bill afterward, together with the blood money. And now detectives Geurts and Sietsema will be in a car, parked close to his front door. They'll be using the van watching the front door through slits. Soon they'll be knocking on his door and if he is silly enough to run to the river and jump into one of the rowboats, he'll be ours. De Gier will start the outboard and we may have him before he has got his oars out, and if de Gier fumbles the State Water Police will catch him. Their launch is right around the next corner and they have a constable under that tree over there, with a pair of binoculars and a radio. The poor silly blighter hasn't got a chance. He'll be back in jail tonight, for another year. They may put him in a special cell for a while. Jailers don't like prisoners who get away. They may play tricks on him. Maybe I should call on him sometime, see that he is all right. Buy him a carton of cigarettes. Grijpstra nodded to himself. Yes. I'll do that.

De Gier was also thinking. He had sucked in his lips and narrowed his eyes. I am a small-time policeman, de Gier was thinking, catching small-time criminals. I should have slipped him a note. De Gier stared at his float, which had moved again although he hadn't seen it move. There would be rain soon, rain and thunder and lightning. The heat was getting oppressive and the color of the clouds had darkened. A great blue heron that had been close to their dinghy, partly hidden by the half-sunk wreck of a river launch, rose slowly into the sky, flapping its large wings. The plume on its thin delicate head moved up as the stately bird started its slow ponderous flight. But he will be caught anyway, de Gier went on thinking. It's a small country and he isn't very intelligent. Can't get away. We know his routine and he can't change his routine. Always the same thing. Find out which way they walk and put a trap on their path. They won't change their paths.

The portable two-way radio that Grijpstra held between his feet squeaked.

"Hello," said Grijpstra.

"Now," the radio said.

"Right."

The detectives pulled in their fishing rods and unscrewed

the parts. De Gier pulled the string on the small outboard engine. It came to life immediately. De Gier allowed it to idle; it made very little noise, puttering gently in the heavy atmosphere of the sultry evening. De Gier smiled. He had expected trouble but the Water Police sergeant who had lent them the boat hadn't exaggerated when he had praised the qualities of the machine.

"Check your pistol," Grijpstra said.

The two pistols—Grijpstra's large model, which he carried in a holster on his belt, and de Gier's light model, which he carried in a special holster in his armpit—clicked as cartridges slid into their barrels.

I won't hit him, de Gier thought. Not even if he runs. I'll outrun him rather.

De Gier will outrun him, Grijpstra thought. He's got long legs.

"There," Grijpstra said.

The man was running through the garden at the back of the house. He jumped into a rowboat moored at the small landing stage.

"Police," Grijpstra shouted. The dinghy was picking up speed. The man was sliding his oars into position.

"Stop," Grijpstra boomed, "you can't get away; there's a launch waiting for you as well. Put up your hands."

The ugly snout of the Water Police launch was edging round the bend in the river.

The man put up his hands. His oars were sliding into the river. Grijpstra lifted one of them out of the water with his left hand.

"Thank you," the man said. "This is my sister's boat. She doesn't want me to lose her oars."

* * *

Geurts and Sietsema were waiting for them in the garden.

"Handcuffs?" Geurts asked.

"No," the man said, "I'll come quietly. I am not armed."

"Let me check," de Gier said, and ran his hands along the man's sides and trouser legs.

"Something in your right pocket," de Gier said. "Show it." It was a clasp knife and de Gier transferred it to his own pocket.

"Thanks, he is yours, Adjutant Geurts."

"Thanks, sergeant."

"Thanks, thanks," the man said. "To you it's work, to me it's a year in jail." He said it pleasantly and Grijpstra smiled.

"Sorry."

"All right, adjutant," the man said. "No hard feelings. But a year is a long time."

"I'll visit you in about a week's time. Anything you want except cigarettes?" Grijpstra said.

The man's eyes grew round. "Are you serious?"

"Of course."

"Some cigars," the man said. "Small cigars. I have an old friend in jail who likes to smoke them."

Grijpstra nodded and waved at the launch of the Water Police, which immediately began to back up, preparing for a U-turn.

De Gier put his pistol back into its holster.

"You always keep your gun in your armpit, sergeant?" the man asked.

"Yes, it doesn't make a bulge that way."

"Very smart," the man said.

"De Gier is a smart cop," Adjutant Geurts said. "Best dressed man on the Force."

There was an awkward silence and Geurts put a hand on the man's shoulder. "Let's go," Geurts said.

De Gier looked into the man's eyes, smiled and touched his arm lightly before turning around. Grijpstra was waiting for him near the van that Adjutant Geurts and Sergeant Sietsema had used to spy on the man's house and that would now transport the prisoner. Grijpstra walked away as de Gier followed him and de Gier had to run to catch up.

"A nice job well done," Grijpstra said heavily.

"What the hell," de Gier said.

"And no fish either," Grijpstra said grumpily. "We were in the boat for more than an hour. I had the right bait and there's plenty of fish out there."

"Bad day," de Gier said.

Their car was parked right at the end of the dike and they had another ten minutes to go. They passed a sleazy café, hidden in a corner of the dike—a shed rather—its crumbly timber badly in need of a coat of paint. Even the metal sign advertising beer was cracked.

"Coffee?" de Gier asked brightly.

Grijpstra nodded. They went inside and sat down at a small table, partly covered by a dirty red and white checked cloth. A teen-age boy was watching them from behind the counter. "Two coffees," de Gier said.

The boy filled two mugs from an archaic machine, which hadn't been polished for years, and spilled some of the sickly looking brownish white fluid as he banged the mugs on the table.

"Why don't you serve it in a bucket?" Grijpstra asked.

The boy shrugged his shoulders and went back to the counter where he picked up a telephone. He had just finished dialing his number when a young woman came rushing into the café and ran straight up to the counter.

"Please let me use the telephone," she said to the boy. "It's an emergency. I want to phone the police."

"Just a minute," the boy said.

"Please, please," the girl shrieked.

De Gier had jumped up. He walked over to the girl and touched her shoulder. "Can I help you, miss? I am a policeman." He showed her his identification but the girl didn't seem to understand.

"Please," she said to the boy. "Give me the telephone."

"What happened, miss?" de Gier asked and tried to show her his identification again but she wasn't paying attention. Grijpstra was amused. The old act, Grijpstra thought, but it'll misfire for once. Watch the wide shoulders, the strong teeth and the charming smile. And the nose, let's not forget the nose. Pity he hasn't had time to comb his hair but perhaps the hair is better in its attractive wild state. It's curling over his ears and there are the little locks on the noble forehead, of course. Pity the lady isn't in the right mood to appreciate it all.

The boy finally put down the phone and the girl frantically dialed the six times two that connects any nervous citizen with the Keepers of the Peace.

De Gier put his hand on the phone. "Miss!" de Gier shouted, "the police are standing right next to you. Detective-Sergeant de Gier, at your service. Now will you tell me what's the matter with you?"

The girl understood. "You are a policeman," she said softly.

"That's right, miss," de Gier said, "and at that little table over there is another policeman: Adjutant-Detective Grijpstra. Come sit with us and tell us what is wrong."

The young woman was pretty and her breathless way of talking and general shyness made her even prettier. She was dressed in a tight pair of faded jeans and a blouse that seemed a little too small to hold her aggressive bouncy breasts. She allowed herself to be led to the table and shook Grijpstra's heavy hand.

"Now," Grijpstra said kindly, "what can we do for you, miss?"

"It's my neighbor," the girl said. "He hasn't been around for a few days and I have been worrying about him." She began to cry.

"Now, now," de Gier said and gave her his handkerchief. The girl sobbed and wiped her eyes.

"And?" Grijpstra asked.

"He never goes out, you see," the girl said. "Only shopping sometimes. He is always back in an hour. And he is always working in his garden. The garden next door to where I live. But I haven't seen him in the garden either and his car is outside, where it always is. Just now I really began to worry and I climbed the fence."

She was sobbing again and Grijpstra patted her on the back. "Yes, miss. Tell us what happened."

"And the door of the kitchen was open and I went upstairs. I had never been in his house before, and there he was."

"He wasn't dead was he?" de Gier asked.

"Yes," the girl shrieked, "he is dead. He's been killed. They've killed him."

"Let's go see," Grijpstra said.

They walked back, almost as far as the house where the escaped prisoner had been caught. The girl stopped in front of a two-storied cottage.

"Is this the house where you found your friend?" Grijpstra asked.

"No," the girl said. "This is where I have a room. We can go through here and then out into the garden."

She opened the door with her key but the two policemen found their way blocked by a short fat woman. "What's all this?" the short woman asked.

"Please let them in, Mary," the girl said. "They are policemen and they want to go next door. Tom is dead."

"Police?" the short woman asked suspiciously, without moving.

De Gier produced his identification and gave it to her. "Sergeant de Gier," the woman read to herself. "Municipal Police, Amsterdam."

"That's right, madam," de Gier said sweetly. "Can we go through your house now?"

His charm didn't impress the woman. She put out a hand and de Gier shook it. He didn't like the feel of the hand. The stubby fingers had a lot of force in them.

"Mary van Krompen," the woman said. "I am a retired teacher and I live here. You can come through if you like, sergeant, though I don't see why you should. Evelien is making a flap about nothing like all young girls do. The man is probably sick or something. How do you know he is dead, Evelien?"

"I *saw* him," Evelien sobbed.

"When?" the short woman asked.

"Just now. I have been inside his house and he's on the floor and there's blood on his face. There's a hole in his face. I am a nurse, aren't I? I *know* when somebody is dead."

"All right, all right," the short woman said.

"Can I come through too?" Grijpstra asked.

"You police too?"

"Yes, madam."

"Any more?"

"No, madam."

"An invasion," Mary muttered. "Wipe your feet, men! I have been cleaning this damned house all day; don't muck it up any more than you have to."

De Gier didn't hear her and Grijpstra didn't answer. They were in the garden and looking at the fence. "You are quite sure that you aren't making all this up, aren't you?" de Gier asked the girl. "If there's nothing the matter with your friend he may be upset if he finds us trampling all over his ground. Legally it would be trespassing and could get us in a lot of trouble."

"Please," the girl said.

De Gier looked at the fence again. It was five feet high and overgrown with creepers. He put his hand on one of its poles. It felt strong enough. "Right," he said and vaulted over. The girl, in spite of her disturbed state of mind, opened her eyes widely. The movement had been perfect, supple and seemingly effortless.

"Wow," the girl said.

Grijpstra sighed and explained, "An athlete; he wins lots of prizes. Has a black belt in judo and is a crack shot too."

The girl, calmed somewhat by the detectives' equanimity, had relaxed a little. "Can you do that too?" she asked, looking at Grijpstra for the first time.

"No," Grijpstra said. "I am bad at sports, but I fish. Unfortunately I don't catch much these days. The water is getting too dirty I think."

There was a faint smile on the girl's face. "Never mind," she said, "I am sure you are a good policeman."

"Middling," Grijpstra said, "but I learn a little every day."

"I am a terrible nurse," the girl said. "I always drop things. I am too nervous."

"You can walk round the fence at the end, Grijpstra," de

Gier called, "near the landing, but be careful or you'll get your feet wet."

Grijpstra maneuvered his heavy body round the fence.

"The window up there is open," de Gier said. "That must be the window of the room where she said she found the body."

The girl joined them.

"Didn't you say the kitchen door was open, miss?" de Gier asked.

She nodded.

"I'll go have a look."

De Gier's head appeared in the upstairs window.

"Yes?" Grijpstra asked.

"Yes," de Gier said. "You'd better come up."

Grijpstra went into the kitchen and found a short flight of stairs at the back and climbed them. De Gier was standing near the slumped body of a young man. The body was, indeed, dead, and lying on its back with both arms stretched out.

"I'll never get used to it, never," de Gier muttered. "Look, his mouth is open and there is a hole between his eyes. A black hole. Bah."

De Gier was very white in the face. He supported himself against the wall.

"Go next door," Grijpstra said, "or, rather, go back to the café. There won't be a telephone next door or the girl would have used it in the first place. I'll wait here. Take the girl home, we don't want too many people running about."

"Yes," de Gier said. There were large wet spots under the arms of his expensive tailored suit.

"Go on," Grijpstra said.

De Gier left. Grijpstra heard him talking to the girl in

the garden. Then the voices faded out. Grijpstra put his
hands in his pockets and looked at the dead man again.
"Silly man," Grijpstra asked, "why did you get yourself
killed?"

||||| 2 |||||

THE THUNDERSTORM TOOK ITS TIME. OCCASIONAL FLASHES
of lightning were followed by thunderclaps, but at long
intervals, and the noise of a heavy truck passing on the dike
behind Grijpstra and the quietly grinning corpse easily swallowed the rumble of far away thunder. The room was dark
and Grijpstra looked about him. There should be a switch
somewhere but he didn't see it. There seemed to be a lot
of furniture in the room. Grijpstra slowly revolved on his
heels. Bookcases, cupboards, a large old-fashioned TV, several easy chairs, two round tables, a couch, a sideboard.
Wherever the wall had offered space a painting had been
hung, paintings with gold frames, frilly frames. The furniture was ornamental as well. There were cushions on the
chairs and the couch—cushions made of thick gleaming
velvet, a tassel on each corner.

Grijpstra moved. He had to find a switch, even if he

would be destroying footmarks and prints. His hands groped along the wall; he stumbled against a chair and hurt his shin. He felt cold and his hands were sweating. His neck itched. The light helped, but not much. A weak bulb illuminated the room, but there were still shadows and the corpse grinned on.

"Silly man," Grijpstra said again.

He sat down on the couch. Why? he asked himself. What had happened? A fight? A disagreement about something? Had the other man threatened the occupant of this rotting, crumbling little hovel? "I'll kill you for that!" Had he shouted? Hissed perhaps? Had he handled the pistol or revolver dramatically, waving it about? Or was this a cold, bam, you-are-dead affair?

Grijpstra told himself to observe. First observe, then draw a conclusion perhaps. No. No conclusion. Observation. What did he observe? A dead man, undoubtedly. A man thirty years old, with thick black hair, a heavy mustache and large white teeth, protruding like a rodent's. No, not a rodent. No mouse or rat. A rabbit. A nice animal. The man looked nice, pleasant, even in death. The grin was horrible, but it was a grin of fear. And surprise. The man had been surprised to meet his death that evening. Evening? Why evening? He might have been shot early in the morning, or in the afternoon. Some time ago now, a day, two days perhaps. Flies had been busy on the face. And the river rats too? No. Grijpstra wiped his face with his large white handkerchief. Not rats. Something strange. What? The furniture. Why would a poor little hovel consisting of a few rooms— a lean-to rather than a house—a shack tottering against the dike, have such a wealth of furniture? There was something else to support this observation. What? Yes; the sports car outside. An expensive new model. The man was a man of property, so why live in a shack? And why was everything so dusty? What else had been dirty? Right, the sports car again. The car was caked over with mud. A year-old car, never cleaned.

He got up so that he could see the corpse better. He wanted to see its clothes. The corpse was wearing a suit: an old-fashioned suit with a waistcoat. No tie. Dirty shirt, frayed collar. He could see one of the cuffs. Frayed too. Old shoes. Grijpstra moved a little. Hole in the sole. A line of logic. Rich man who doesn't look after himself. Yes. Look at that enormous easy chair facing the TV. Probably the only chair the man ever sat in. Watching TV. Grijpstra saw the ashtray. Filled with stubs, ash, crumpled empty cigarette packs. The ashtray had overflowed. Empty beer cans too. No glasses, just cans. How many? Grijpstra counted and stopped at fifty; there would be more. A very untidy man. No. Something didn't click again. What was it? Yes. The garden. He took a step forward and could see the garden through the open windows. A beautiful garden. Neat rows of dahlias, daisies, asters. Shrubs at the side. The cobblestones under the tree had been swept and the garden chair looked clean as well. What had the girl said? "Always in the garden." So—neat outside, messy inside. Crazy. Why?

But there was something else that didn't click. Where was de Gier?

"Grijpstra," de Gier said. He was standing in the open door.

"Yes?"

"They'll be a while. I telephoned but I couldn't locate anyone except the sergeant at the desk. They are all over the town. There was a corpse in the canal, and a corpse in the park, and there has been a fight in a pub somewhere. The doctor is busy and the photographers are and the fingerprint people too. We may have to wait some time. The chief inspector is off duty; his mother is very ill. The commissaris will come. He is visiting friends and they couldn't reach him straight off."

"No," Grijpstra said. "What about the famous city service? There should be two cars racing around, two cars full of officers. Inspectors and subinspectors. Where are they?"

"Busy," de Gier said. "It's a hot evening."

"Well, sit down," Grijpstra said. "This is a funny place. Look around."

"Grijpstra," de Gier said.

"No. Let me think. I was thinking something when you came in and now it's gone again."

Grijpstra closed his eyes and the heavy eyebrows came down and almost hid the sockets of his eyes. He frowned and his hands became big powerful fists. What? Ah, yes. The hole. The bullet hole. Right between the eyes. Not a scorched wound, so there had been a fair distance between gun muzzle and victim's head. A good shot. A very good shot. An excellent shot, considering that the dead man must have been standing close to the window, looking out. And the killer was in the garden. A crack shot. Professional. That had been the thought that flitted through his slow dense brain. Nobody carries firearms in Holland. To carry a firearm is a crime. Even an unloaded gun in a man's pocket draws a heavy fine and a stretch in jail. To threaten with a toy gun is a crime. Nobody gets a license to carry arms. For sport, yes. But only to take the gun, suitably wrapped up, directly from one's house to the shooting club, and straight back again. And even a sporting license is hard to get. There are forms to be filled in, and memberships to be obtained, and the police want references. But here a man had been shot, from a distance, and right between the eyes.

A gangster? And why, pray, would a gangster shoot a man who works in his garden during the day and who watches his TV in the evening? A man who doesn't even work? Who only goes out to do a little shopping? Grijpstra groaned. What had they stumbled into now? Into a maniac who hides a horrible secret and another maniac comes and kills him from the garden? No. Amsterdam is a quiet town. A nice quiet town. Grijpstra had spent the afternoon reading through police reports covering nearly three full weeks of daily events. Thefts, burglaries, a few street robberies, a knife fight, suicides, plenty of fires, a house that had collapsed of old age and crushed the leg of a child. The worst that had happened during the last two *months* had been an Italian bankrobber trying to fire an ancient Sten gun, which had jammed after the third cartridge. The police never stopped talking about it. "Tommy guns," the young constables had said in the canteens. "It'll be cannon next and all we have is 7.65 pistols with six cartridges." The officers had smiled at the constables, patted their heads and said, "Now, now, now." And here was a man with a hole between his eyes.

"Grijpstra," de Gier said again.

"Yes, yes."

"He was shot from the garden," de Gier said, "through the open window."

"I know."

"Look at all those empty beer cans."

"I have seen them."

"This is an antique shop," de Gier said. "Where did he get all this stuff? It's valuable too. If the whole house is filled with this type of furniture, he must have owned a hundred thousand guilders' worth of antiques. So why didn't he get someone to clean up for him? And why didn't he polish his shoes? Or get a new color TV instead of that croaky old thing? Or buy a shirt?"

"Yes," Grijpstra said.

"Crazy," de Gier said. "A crazy man. And why kill him?"

"And why be neat in the garden and sloppy in the house?" Grijpstra asked.

"I don't know," de Gier said. "I'm sloppy on the balcony and neat in the house. Other way around. But not as sloppy as this bird."

"He looks like a rabbit," Grijpstra said, "not a bird."

"A rabbit?" de Gier asked and stood up so that he could see the face of the dead man. He sat down again. "Yes. Harmless sort of face. So what do we do now?"

"Wait," Grijpstra said, "and remember to keep people from tramping about in the garden. There should be some prints out there. I would think that he stood over there, right in front of the open windows, and that the killer stood in the garden. The killer must have called him and fired as soon as he showed himself."

"It has begun to rain," de Gier said gloomily, "and it rained yesterday. This corpse may be a few days old." He sniffed, and got white in the face again.

Grijpstra sniffed too. "A bit of a smell, not much. The windows were open of course."

"There may still be prints," de Gier said, "somewhere where the rain couldn't get at them to wipe them out."

"There'll be something," Grijpstra said in a soothing voice, as if he wanted to reassure not only de Gier but himself as well. He felt tired and stupid and he didn't want a difficult case to work on. The summer had been hot so far and the small house on the Lijnbaansgracht, where he lived with his fat wife and three noisy children, had exhausted him. The endless variety show that his TV poured out evening after evening had worn his nerves down to thin infected threads. There had been a lot of loud fights with his wife. Whenever he switched the set off she switched it on again. There had been no escape. The voices of the comics, the bad men and the good men of the crime films, the quiz masters and the newscasters had followed him to the small bedroom. His wife liked to put the volume up. She was getting deaf. I'll be deaf too; soon I'll be deaf, Grijpstra thought hopelessly. He had a vision of a quiet room somewhere else, a room without TV, and with a view of the river. He could sit in that room and watch the boats coming past. Lovely. No wife. He saw the plastic curlers in her hair and shuddered. No more women in his life. He would read the paper and paint in his free time. And de Gier could come visit him sometimes and they might play music together, and then de Gier would go and he would have the room all to himself again. No wife. No TV. But there would still be the children. He would take them for walks during the weekends, especially the two little ones, and his wife would screech at him from the open house door. She might come to Police Headquarters and screech at him there. She had done it before, after he had been away for a few days once. He had been working at the time but she thought that he had left her. He felt his face go red with shame. It had been the most horrible scene of his life. The commissaris had saved him that time. He had talked to the hysterical woman and got her out of Grijpstra's room into the corridor and eventually out of the building. De Gier had been embarrassed, de Gier and the other detectives who had been forced witnesses to the scene. Grijpstra jumped. Someone had rung the bell.

"I'll go," de Gier said. "About time too."

"Evening," the commissaris said to Grijpstra. "What have we found now?"

"He's over there, sir," Grijpstra said. The corpse was hidden from the commissaris by a table, covered with a thick oriental rug that hung down to the floor.

"Ah," the commissaris said and bent down. He studied the appearance and the position of the dead man, and glanced up at the open windows.

The bell rang again and de Gier opened the door to two policemen in uniform. There were a lot of people running about on the dike now and some of them began to talk to de Gier, asking him what had happened.

"Whoever lives here is dead," de Gier said to the crowd. "Does anyone know the man?"

There was no answer. The faces stared at the tall handsome detective wearing a blue denim suit. They were studying the stranger who had projected himself into their routine. They noted the curly hair, the blue eyes and the delicate hawk's nose. De Gier looked back at them and was reminded of a painting by Brueghel. The faces he saw seemed to belong to nitwits, idiots. The man closest to him was wearing torn black corduroy trousers and a dirty shirt, open and showing the gray hairs on his thin chest. There were no hairs on the shining skull, gleaming in the electric light of the dike; and the toothless mouth was a dark hole below the bulbous nose, puffed and violet by a million glasses of raw jenever that had oozed through its veins. The man inspired little confidence but he was, de Gier thought, perhaps the best of the small crowd facing him.

"You," de Gier said, touching the man on the shoulder, "do you know the man who lived here?"

"I know his name," the man said, "Tom Wernekink is his name."

"Lived here long?" de Gier asked.

"A year maybe, or longer. Not much longer. He bought the house when the fellow who lived in it before was taken away."

"Jail?"

"No. The madhouse. Old granddad who did a bit of drinking." The toothless mouth tittered. "Ambulance took him away and he never came back. His children sold the house. Too cheap. I heard the price later. Should have bought it myself. Houses are worth a lot of money nowadays."

"Was he working?" de Gier asked. "This Tom Wernekink? Did he ever have a job?"

The little fellow was shaking his head. "No. He was always here, in his garden. Maybe he was collecting unemployment benefits. He went away in his car sometimes but he was always right back again."

"Did you ever talk to him?"

"No. He didn't talk. Said good morning and good afternoon, that was all he said."

"OK," de Gier said, wondering why he was wasting his time. He could always ask the girl with the nice breasts who lived next door.

"If anyone has any information that may help us, please leave your name and address with the constables here," he said in a loud voice, addressing the crowd. He turned to the two uniformed policemen. "You'd better stay here and guard the door. There'll be more cars coming in a minute. There is a dead man inside. Perhaps somebody knows something. You can call me if you think you should; I'll be inside or in the house next door."

"Did he cop a bullet?" one of the constables asked.

"Yes, right between the eyes."

"Look for his wife or his girlfriend, sergeant," the constable said. "I have a collection of newspaper articles at home; whenever there is a crime in the paper I clip it out. I was reading through all the manslaughter stuff I have the other day and every time it seems to be the husband or the wife or the lover, especially in Amsterdam. Strange, isn't it?"

"My wife wouldn't kill me," the other constable said.

"Why not?"

"Well, I work for her, don't I?"

"You also irritate her," the constable said, "and you are always around. Every evening, the weekends, the holidays."

De Gier laughed.

"You don't agree, sergeant?" the constable asked.

"Sure," de Gier said, "but I was thinking that I haven't got a wife."

"Girlfriends do it too," the constable said.

"I haven't got a girlfriend right now," de Gier said, "but I think I irritate my cat. Look." He showed a deep scratch on his wrist.

"Exactly," the constable said. "Proves my theory. Your cat gets frustrated, or depressed, or just a little crazy, and who does he attack? You. You are the first thing in his way so he goes for you."

"Good reasoning, constable," de Gier said. "I'll keep it in mind."

"Probably read it somewhere," the other constable said, and posted himself at the door, legs astride and clasped hands on his back. He straightened himself and looked at the crowd from under his cap.

"All right, get going, get going," the other constable shouted. "Don't obstruct the road. Nothing to see here now."

The police cars finally arrived and the investigation followed its normal course with special attention paid to the garden where two men wandered around holding powerful torches. Some footprints were found and soon the men were kneeling in the wet earth, building boxes out of metal foil, sprinkling gypsum powder into a bucket and stirring the mixture carefully, muttering at the photographers who were also interested in the prints.

De Gier looked for Grijpstra and found him upstairs in the loft where the commissaris was sitting on an unmade bed. "I agree, Grijpstra," the commissaris was saying. "Our friend didn't look after himself much. Dirty sheets, unswept floor, full ashtrays, beer cans everywhere. Did you find a bathroom or a shower anywhere?"

"No, sir."

"So he must have washed and shaved in the kitchen sink. But he was rich, undoubtedly. I was looking at that antique rosewood desk downstairs, a collector's piece. I'm sure it's worth a small fortune. And the china collection in the cupboard is worth a fortune too. Yet he didn't seem to care for the stuff. He didn't even bother to place the furniture properly. It looks as if the movers plunked it down and that's where it stayed. Let's look for his papers; maybe they'll tell us something."

Grijpstra and de Gier began to open drawers and cupboard doors. They found clothes, dirty clothes mostly. "The doctor is probably finished with the body now," Grijpstra said. "He should have a wallet in his jacket." The commissaris negotiated the narrow staircase carefully. Grijpstra clomped down and de Gier, after a last look around the loft, followed him.

"Evening," the commissaris said to the doctor and shook hands. "Any idea how long he has been dead?"

"Some time," the doctor said. "I'll have to do my tests but I would think that the bullet got him at least two days ago. It'll be difficult to determine the exact time; the longer the body lies around the harder the case becomes. I'll tell you tomorrow."

"Can I go through his pockets?" de Gier asked.

"Sure."

"Let me do it," Grijpstra said. "You'll faint and we don't want more work for the doctor."

"Thanks," de Gier said.

The commissaris smiled. De Gier had fainted before—twice in fact—and both times when confronted by a corpse, but fainting is not unusual in the police. And de Gier wouldn't faint when he had to be active in some way—run, or shoot, or think.

"Here," Grijpstra said, and gave the wallet to the commissaris.

The commissaris looked through its contents. He studied the passport, which showed rubber stamps indicating three trips to England, each trip lasting exactly two weeks. Holidays, the commissaris thought. There was also an address in Kralingen, a suburb of Rotterdam. The address was crossed out and a new address given as 131, Landsburger dike, Amsterdam North. The change of address had been countersigned by a clerk of the mayor's office. "Office employee," the commissaris said aloud; "so he does have a job, or he did have a job anyway. And he is thirty-one years old. Thomas Wernekink. Well, well. We still know nothing." There was a driver's license in the wallet, four hundred guilders and a slip from the bank showing that he had 28,000 guilders in his current account.

"A lot of money," Grijpstra said.

"There may be even more," the commissaris said. "This is his current account; he may have a savings account as well. We'll check with the bank tomorrow. Banks usually know something about their clients and he is banking with a small branch office. The Rotterdam police should be very helpful, they always are. We have his old address in Kralingen; isn't that a very expensive suburb?"

"Yes, sir," Grijpstra said, "lots of villas and a big park and some exclusive blocks of flats facing the park. There's a lake, a nice lake—people go sailing there."

"Some information anyway," the commissaris said. "We'll go into it tomorrow. Anything else we should do here?"

"We could go talk to the girl next door," de Gier said, "the girl who asked us to take a look here. She seemed to be in love with Wernekink but he never even asked her in, so she won't know much. Still..."

"All right." The commissaris tried to look brisk and businesslike but all he really wanted to do was to go home and have a very hot bath. His legs were bothering him and the hot water would soak the pain out of his bones. "All right, let's go next door."

The door opened the minute de Gier put his finger on the bell. "Good evening," the commissaris said to the short fat woman who had introduced herself earlier to de Gier as Mary van Krompen. "We would like to ask a few questions to a young lady who lives here, I believe. Do you mind if we come in?"

The woman stared at the commissaris. "Well..." she said, "it's pretty late. Can't you come back tomorrow? We would like to go to bed."

"Please, madam," the commissaris said gently, "we are police officers and there has been a crime next door. A man has been shot dead; we would like to apprehend the killer and perhaps the young lady and yourself can help us."

Mary van Krompen weakened. The commissaris looked very harmless and kind. "Come in," she said gruffly. They were led into a sitting room and the woman stamped off to find the girl.

Their surroundings were very different now. The room was light and clean and the general appearance of the house was pleasant enough. Some effort had been made to restore the old building but the beams supporting the ceiling had been left as they had been for several hundred years, their dark color setting off the white walls. There were fresh flowers on the table and potted plants on the windowsills. A row of silver trophies were displayed on a corner table, some eight silver cups, varying in size. Grijpstra got up to admire them. "I say," Grijpstra said, "you know what these are?" The commissaris and de Gier joined him. De Gier picked up one of the cups and studied it. The cup was decorated with two crossed revolvers.

"Shooting trophies," the commissaris said.

They were still looking at the trophies when Mary van Krompen came back, bringing the girl with her.

"Evelien Dapper," the girl said to the three men, "that's my name. You want to see me?"

"Yes, dear," the commissaris said, "please sit down. We know you are very upset but you discovered the body and you knew the man, so you can be very helpful to our investigation."

The girl sniffed.

"Please tell us what you know," the commissaris said gently.

"I've already told the other men," the girl said and crumpled her handkerchief into a hard little ball. "I was worried about Tom so I went into his house and there he was, on the floor."

"Yes. You had never been in his house before?"

"No," Mary said suddenly and glared at the commissaris.

"They used to whisper to each other over the fence and she gave him cups of tea."

"We *didn't* whisper," the girl said indignantly. "We just talked and he was always very nice. We were neighbors, weren't we, and he never did anything for himself except digging about in his garden; so why shouldn't I make him a cup of tea sometimes?"

"Quite, quite," the commissaris said, smiling at Mary. "Why shouldn't she? But he never asked you in?"

"No," the girl said.

"But that's strange, isn't it? You are an attractive girl and he was a young man, and you got to know each other. How long did you know him?"

"As long as I've lived here," the girl said. "Three months now, I think."

Mary laughed and the commissaris gave her a puzzled look. "Sorry," Mary said. "I don't want to be unpleasant but I have been wondering myself. Here they were, every afternoon, chatting away and sipping their tea and he never even thought of asking her in."

"A very shy young man perhaps," the commissaris said.

The girl began to cry again and de Gier felt guilty. He remembered how he had ignored her tears and stuttered questions when earlier they left the house for Wernekink's. He had been mumbling at her instead of saying something helpful.

He remembered the lessons in police philosophy at school. It is the task of the police to actively maintain order and to assist those who are in need of help. The girl had been in need of help but he hadn't even listened to her; he had been too busy trying to suppress his own fear and nausea. And he shuddered when he remembered coming back from the café telephone. The dike had been filled with small groups of people, clustered together in the eerie reflection of street-lights swinging in a storm that had chosen that moment to swoop down from the great inland lake. An old man had stopped him to ask what was going on in Tom Wernekink's house. He hadn't answered and the old man had leered at him. "A bit of work for you today, hey, state pimp? Finally have to do something in return for all that lovely tax money?" The words "state pimp" had made de Gier stop but he had forced himself to go on.

"It's no use asking her anything, commissaris," Mary said, "or me for that matter. We didn't know the boy really."

"Please sit down, ladies," the commissaris said. Mary flopped down on the nearest chair and Evelien sat down on the edge of a couch.

But what could I have said to the girl? de Gier thought. The boy was dead, wasn't he? He wasn't just dead; he was rotting. Should I have said that he had passed away, gone to a better world?

"Who else lives here, madam?" the commissaris asked.

"My girlfriend," Mary said, "Ann Helders; she isn't here now; she's on night duty. She's a nurse."

Lesbian, Grijpstra and de Gier were thinking simulta-neously. It was the way Mary had said, "my girlfriend." The words had sounded possessive and defiant. It seemed as if Mary was challenging the men. I live with a girl, so what? I am proud of it. I haven't got a man, and I don't want a man. Men are dirt.

The commissaris was looking at the grim expression on the woman's face. She hasn't discovered yet that it's all right to be lesbian, the commissaris was thinking. She is of my generation. To be different is to be shameful. Times have changed. But we don't catch up anymore; some ideas have seeped in too deeply—nothing can dislodge them anymore.

"I see," the commissaris said. "Did any of you hear the shot? The man was shot, you see, and we think he was shot from the garden."

"The garden?" Mary asked. "When was he shot? Do you know that too?"

"No," the commissaris said. "Two days ago perhaps but we don't know the time. We should know tomorrow when the doctor has finished his tests."

"I didn't hear a shot," Mary said; "did you, Evelien?"

The girl was trying not to cry. She shook her head.

"Did you know your neighbor, Miss van Krompen?" the commissaris asked.

"Hardly. He wasn't a talkative man. We exchanged a few words when we were both working in our gardens but that's all. The weather, I think that's all we ever talked about, the weather."

"Did he have any friends?"

"Don't think so. The Cat with Boots On sometimes came to see him. He lived farther down, on the dike. I don't know his real name. We all call him Cat. He's a crazy-looking man."

"Ah," the commissaris said, "so he did have one friend at least. Where does this Cat live?"

Mary had closed her eyes and was counting. "Seventh house on the left from here."

"We'll go see him later," the commissaris said. "Is there anything else you know that you think you should tell us?"

"No," Mary said.

The commissaris looked at Evelien. "You? Miss Dapper?"

The girl was still crying.

"Miss Dapper?"

She got up and rushed from the room.

"Hmm," the commissaris said.

"I'll make some coffee," Mary said, "powdered coffee; it'll only take a few minutes. Do you all take milk and sugar?"

"Please," the three men said.

When Mary left the room Grijpstra got up and began to look at the trophies again.

"Are you thinking what I am thinking?" de Gier asked Grijpstra.

"What are you thinking, de Gier?" the commissaris asked softly.

"Just a combination of some half-observed facts, sir," de Gier said.

"Go ahead."

"Mary is a lesbian," de Gier said. "She lives with this nurse—Ann Helders, I believe the name was. But Ann brings a friend into the house who becomes a lodger. Our young pretty lady who rushed out of the room just now. Evelien. Mary falls in love with Evelien but can't show her love because of Ann. The result is frustration. Mary is a violent woman. Her favorite sport is pistol shooting. Violent sports are usually a release for built-up tension. The love of arms points at aggression. A violent and aggressive woman. Evelien starts flirting with the neighbor, a man. Mary doesn't like that. The flirting goes on and on. Everyday Evelien makes tea for Tom Wernekink and gives him a cup across the fence. They drink the tea together and laugh and chat and Mary watches it all from the house and boils with fury. She can't kill Evelien because she loves her but she can remove Tom, so one day she sneaks out into the garden next door, calls Tom and shoots him, right between the eyes."

"As easy as that, what?" Grijpstra asked.

"Weren't you thinking along the same lines as you were fiddling about with that cup just now?" de Gier asked.

Grijpstra grunted.

They both looked at the commissaris who had lit a small cigar and was puffing away thoughtfully. "Could be," the commissaris said slowly. "It explains the shot between the eyes. I tried to work out the distance between pistol, and wound; tomorrow we'll have exact figures, but I would think the distance must have been some twenty-five to thirty feet. To hit a man between the eyes, with a pistol, at that distance, is a rare feat. And Mary has won a lot of cups."

"The psychology I put into my theory is a bit rough," de Gier said. "There must have been more than just frustration about a few cups of tea. Maybe they aren't being too truthful with us. Perhaps Tom Wernekink came here often and slept with the girl. Perhaps they were having a proper affair. Mary was threatening the girl and now the girl is too frightened to say anything. It could be that Mary is waving a pistol at the girl right now."

"Go and look," the commissaris said. "Pretend you want to help her bring in the coffee."

De Gier got up and left the room. He found Mary peacefully engaged in the small kitchen in the back of the house.

"You carry the tray," Mary said. "Sergeant, isn't it? Should I call you sergeant?"

"Call me anything you like," de Gier said.

Mary's voice sounded fairly pleasant but when he looked at her face he saw that the muscles were working and that she was biting her thin lips.

"What do you do for a living, madam?" the commissaris asked.

"I used to teach."

"What?"

"Mathematics at a high school."

"So you have a degree," the commissaris said.

"I have."

The commissaris stirred his coffee.

"Did you win all these trophies?" Grijpstra asked.

"I did."

"So you are a crack shot," de Gier said. "Your neighbor was shot between the eyes, from a fair distance."

Mary put her cup down with a bang. "Meaning what?"

"We try to apply logic when we think, madam," the commissaris said. "Very few people could hit a man between the eyes from a distance of twenty-five or thirty feet. I have calculated a little and I think that the distance must be about that. I would have trouble to score under such circumstances and I spend a lot of time target shooting. Very few people I know can shoot well enough to equal the performance in your neighbor's garden. You are a crack shot. You are also a mathematician."

"I didn't shoot him," Mary said.

"De Gier," the commissaris said, "go next door and find out if they have succeeded in making clear plaster prints in the garden. If they have bring them here."

"Sir," de Gier said, and left the room.

"Now," the commissaris said to the woman, "if you don't mind we would like to see all your shoes."

"Don't you need a warrant for a request like that?" Mary asked.

"I am a commissaris; I don't need a warrant."

"I see," Mary said and looked at the two men grimly.

"If you find that my shoes have left prints in the garden next door..." Mary said.

"We would have another indication."

"Commissaris," Mary said slowly, "I may have been in that garden quite often, for perfectly harmless reasons."

"No," the commissaris said, "you, and Evelien as well, have told us that your neighbor didn't welcome visitors. He wouldn't even allow a nice attractive young lady who obviously liked him to join him in his garden. He drank the tea she gave him but he stayed on his side of the fence. Correct?"

"Yes."

"So why should he allow you to go into his garden? He wouldn't, would he?"

"He wouldn't," Mary said. "You don't have to go through the rigmarole of the shoes," she added. "I admit that I have been in his garden."

"When?"

"Yesterday. I was wondering what had happened to him and I wanted to shut up Evelien, who was moping about the house, worrying."

"And did you see him?"

"Yes, I stood on a box and looked through the window. He was dead. Shot."

"Why didn't you call the police?"

"Because they would think what they are thinking now."

"That you shot him?"

Mary nodded, her square heavy head bobbed up and down. "Exactly. And I didn't shoot him. Why should I?"

"Jealousy, perhaps," Grijpstra said.

Mary laughed dryly. "Why jealousy? Ann is my girl-friend, not Evelien. If the silly girl wants to play about with men that's her business, isn't it? And she wasn't even successful. He would drink her tea and that was all. What was it to me?"

"You may have a great liking for Evelien," the commissaris said. "She is a beautiful girl."

"I already have a girlfriend, and I am happy with her and she with me. Why should I run after others?"

"I don't know why people should do things," the commissaris said; "the fact is that they do."

The commissaris made a sign to Grijpstra. "Excuse me, madam," Grijpstra said. "I'll go tell de Gier that the prints are no longer necessary."

"Tell me," the commissaris said, looking over the rim of his coffee cup, "we are alone now and nobody will overhear us. Did you shoot that young man or didn't you?"

Mary got up and rearranged the trophies on the corner table. "I did not."

"Do you realize that we have to arrest you?" the commissaris asked pleasantly.

"By logic, yes. I agree with you that very few people would be able to aim that accurately. One in a hundred thousand perhaps."

The fat woman looked desperate. The commissaris didn't take his eyes off the square face opposite him. He was looking at her eyes, large pale blue eyes, slightly bulging behind the thick curved glasses of her spectacles. He wanted to tell her to relax, not to suffer more than she had to, but he couldn't find any purpose in saying anything. Mary van Krompen's situation was decidedly uncomfortable and there was very little he could do about it. She was upset, nervous, anxious and probably quite frightened. All he could do was try not to aggravate her any further. It would be awkward if de Gier and Grijpstra had to drag her into the police car.

"The pistol," Mary said suddenly; "surely you have a

ballistics department in your Headquarters. You have, haven't you?"

"Yes," the commissaris said.

"Well, they can prove that the bullet didn't come from any of my pistols. I have two, a 7.65 and a .22. I know the bullet didn't come from either one and your people can confirm that it didn't."

"Yes," the commissaris said. "You better give me your weapons."

Mary laughed, a harsh grating laugh. "Give me your weapons! Aren't you afraid that the killer-woman will take a pop at you as well? I would wait a little, if I were you."

"Wait for what?" the commissaris asked, surprised.

"For your two gorillas to arrive. That big burly fellow and the handsome charmer."

The commissaris grinned. "Gorillas!"

Suddenly Mary laughed too. "A gorilla and a gibbon I should have said. The thin chappie looks quite agile, with his long arms and fine face. He could swing himself through the trees; it would be a dainty sight."

Mary and the commissaris were giggling together when the two detectives returned and Grijpstra raised his eyebrows at de Gier.

"The lady wants to give us her two pistols," the commissaris said to Grijpstra. "Go with her and collect them please, and take the ammunition as well."

Mary kept her pistols in the drawer of her nightstand. The arms were wrapped in flannel and looked in excellent repair. "Careful," Mary said as Grijpstra slipped them into the pockets of his jacket, "they are precision instruments, both of them, and I have spent many hours cleaning them."

"Yes, miss," Grijpstra said politely, "and the ammo please." He was given two cartons. "Thank you, miss."

"Can I pack a few things in a suitcase?" Mary asked. "Your chief wants to arrest me. I am innocent of course, but I am sure you'll keep me there for a long while. A prisoner has no rights I believe."

"You won't be a prisoner, madam," Grijpstra said. "You are a suspect and suspects have all sorts of rights. We'll look after you as best we can."

"Yes," Mary said bitterly, "you won't let me smoke and you won't let me read and I'll sit in a small concrete cubbyhole for hours and hours on end. I have heard stories."

"You'll be all right, miss," Grijpstra said, and watched the woman pack pyjamas, books, cigarettes and toilet gear into a battered overnight bag.

When Mary faced the commissaris again she stopped. "Commissaris," she said firmly.

"Yes, miss?"

"I assure you I am innocent and I promise you I won't run away. My word of honor. Don't take me with you. If you want me you can send a message and I'll be with you within thirty minutes. I'll take a cab if necessary although I don't have much money. But I don't want to go into a police cell. Please." Her underlip was trembling and both Grijpstra and de Gier looked away.

The commissaris sighed and put a thin old man's hand on the fat woman's shoulder. "Believe me, I have to take you with me. All indications point at you. Your prints are in the garden. You failed to inform the police when you discovered the corpse. You are a crack shot and our man has been killed by a crack shot. Very few people know how to handle firearms. There may be a motive. It all adds up to grave suspicion. It is very possible that you are guilty of the most serious crime we know in our law books. If I don't take you with me I will be guilty of negligence. It's all very logical; surely you see what I am driving at?"

"And there is no pity in the law?" Mary asked, her underlip still trembling.

"Yes," the commissaris said gravely, "there is pity in the law. There may be many faults in the way this country runs its affairs but the law is compassionate. But not at this stage of the investigation. We have to arrest you and put you into a cell..."

"All right," Mary said, "take me then, but you'd better tell Evelien; she's upstairs."

The commissaris nodded at de Gier. Grijpstra opened the door for Mary and waved at the uniformed driver in the commissaris' car.

"Do you want me to come with you, sir?"

"No, Grijpstra," the commissaris said. "I'll see you at nine o'clock in my office tomorrow. Wait for de Gier and go home; you can tell the two constables guarding Wernekink's house to go home as well. The body has been removed and there is nothing else to do over there." The commissaris stepped back and Mary got into the black Citroën. The driver saluted as he helped her into the car.

⫾⫾⫾⫾ 3 ⫾⫾⫾⫾

THE RED LIGHT ATTACHED TO THE COMMISSARIS' OFFICE door was on and his telephone was, temporarily, disconnected. No one, except the chief constable—who could press a special button that engaged a buzzer near the commissaris' desk—could disturb him now. The commissaris was facing his three visitors. "Yes," the commissaris said, addressing the public prosecutor, a man in his late forties, conservatively dressed in a dark blue suit, white shirt and gray tie, "I know this isn't usual procedure but I asked these two detectives in because I value their insight and advice."

The public prosecutor nodded, Grijpstra smiled and de Gier looked noncommittal. "I appreciate the company of the two gentlemen," the public prosecutor said slowly, "and the matter is serious enough. We are, after all, trying to reach a decision about the liberty of a human being, and liberty is the greatest good."

"Yes," the commissaris said quietly.

"But there's something about this I don't like so much," the public prosecutor said, and the laugh wrinkles around his eyes suddenly became very noticeable.

"Yes?" the commissaris asked.

"It seems that I am being asked what *I* think about the possible guilt of Miss Mary van Krompen," the public prosecutor said. "Your approach should have been different. You should have tried to *prove* the guilt of the lady to me. You have been questioning her now for two days and you can't hold her any longer on your own authority. All right. So now my office has to approve her remaining in custody. Fine. The police tell us about their suspicions, the various facts are outlined, we read through the reports of the interrogators, and we make up our mind."

"Yes?" the commissaris asked.

"Yes. But this time you ask *me* what I think. Are you in doubt about what you should do?"

The commissaris nodded gravely. "Yes, I am in doubt. Very much so."

"Why? The facts seem clear enough. Footprints, nice clear plaster of Paris footprints matching the lady's shoes. The lady admits that she saw the corpse but she didn't contact the police; that's a crime in itself and I hope you'll charge her with it. And on top of it all the unbelievable accuracy of the shot. A thirty-three-foot distance between weapon and wound according to the experts and the victim didn't just stand there waiting to be shot between the eyes. He must have moved when he realized his life was in danger. the killer can't have had more than a few seconds to pull the trigger. Wernekink wasn't tied to a stake was he, or blindfolded?" The public prosecutor was working himself

up into a rage, acting his part at court, facing the judges
and the lawyer defending the accused.

"Ah, hum," the public prosecutor said, "excuse me, I
was being carried away by the clear implications of the
evidence facing us. Still, the evidence *is* undeniable, isn't
it? And the lady is a crack shot; she won a number of prizes
and she is the champion of her club."

"Yes, sir," the commissaris said, "she is a champion; she
is also a lesbian, and the girl making up to the neighbor—
a girl living in her house as a lodger—is very attractive.
But there is no conclusive evidence, I think. No, not conclusive. The lady swears she didn't do it. She holds a master's degree in mathematics and she admits that the chance
that another crack shot got our friend is very small. But the
chance does exist, we must admit it. There are, after all,
other people who know how to handle a gun, even in Holland. De Gier, for instance. De Gier, do you think you could
manage a perfect shot like that?"

De Gier sat up. "Perhaps," he said. "I have had some
very good results in the shooting gallery, and I have also
been reasonably successful outside. Last year I hit a running
robber in the leg at a sixty-foot distance and it was dark,
and I had been running before I stopped to fire. But I think
it was a fluke shot."

"Yes, yes," the commissaris said impatiently, "we know
about that. The question is whether you could have hit a
man between the eyes at a thirty-three-foot distance? With
one shot, mind you; we only found one empty cartridge in
the garden."

De Gier was shaking his head. "I can't say yes or no,
sir. I might be able to do it but there are always circumstances. The wind, the weapon, my state of nerves. I can
never hit anything after I have been riding my bicycle; it

seems that the vibration of a cycle affects the muscles of my arm."

"There must be other crack shots in Holland," the public prosecutor said, "and perhaps Sergeant de Gier is one of them. We also have to weigh the fact that the bullet wasn't fired from either of the two pistols that the lady owns and that she surrendered to you."

"No," Grijpstra said, "I don't think the point weakens our suspicion. Guns are for sale, aren't they? And members of shooting clubs can get guns easier than others. The people who repair guns often sell arms on the sly. They can buy parts and a full set of parts is a complete gun. And it's very easy to buy firearms in Belgium. If Mary wanted to buy a gun she could buy one, and if she wanted to remove Tom Wernekink she wouldn't kill him with one of her own guns."

"So?" the public prosecutor asked. "I think your evidence is heavy enough; you can hold her for another two days as far as I am concerned. I have said it before, but you don't seem very pleased."

"Yes, yes, yes," the commissaris muttered, "but I had a second reason to ask for your opinion. You are a doctor of law and a skilled lawyer; you have a different sort of brain, not a police brain as I have. We are investigators but we never judge."

"I am not a judge," the public prosecutor said. "I prosecute, that's a different discipline altogether."

"I know, I know," the commissaris said, "but still, your angle is different. I am not convinced about the lady's guilt. Her denials are very straightforward. She isn't a devious woman either; she is used to saying what she thinks."

"Do you like her?" the public prosecutor asked.

The commissaris got up and began bending his knees

and straightening up again. "Yes," he said slowly, "I think I like her."

The public prosecutor looked around, trying to make contact with the three policemen. The commissaris was staring at the wall, Grijpstra was staring out the window and de Gier had closed his eyes. The public prosecutor got up and waved his hands. "Look here," he said, "what the hell do you want of me? Aren't you exaggerating the importance of my office? All I can do is give permission twice to hold a suspect for two days. I admit that the first request is no more than a formality; if a police commissaris tells me that he suspects a person of having committed a serious crime I will allow him to hold the suspect for two days for questioning. The second request is more serious and I go into the matter. I *did* go into this matter. I saw your lady, I weighed the evidence, I really studied the case. So all right, you have another two days. But what is another two days? Forty-eight hours pass pretty quickly, don't they? She isn't all that uncomfortable in her cell, is she? Why don't you wait for the judge? If she still hasn't convinced you of her innocence after another two days, the judge has to decide. Wait for the judge!"

"Another two days," the commissaris said softly.

"So what the hell?" the public prosecutor said, getting red in the face.

"It isn't just that I like her," the commissaris said; "there's something else."

The public prosecutor sighed. "That's better. Tell me about it."

"We laughed together," the commissaris said.

"Laughed?" said Grijpstra. "So that's what it was? When de Gier and I had been out of the room? I thought I noticed something when I came back, in fact I thought that she had given in."

"No, no. She never gave in. But something funny happened and I laughed and she laughed with me. Suddenly she became relaxed, normal, pleasant even."

"Funny?" de Gier asked. "What were you and the lady laughing about, sir?"

"Never mind."

Grijpstra grinned. "Must have been something about you, de Gier; I am never funny."

The mustache of the public prosecutor began to bristle. "What's all this now? So she laughed, so something funny happened, so what?"

"Fear and amusement do not go together," the commissaris said.

The public prosecutor's mood changed. He remembered the many conversations he had had with the commissaris, both at Headquarters and at home. He also remembered his admiration for the frail old man who so often approached a problem from an unusual, but often correct, angle. He sighed again. "Well, we'll have to go on with her. We can't let her go. I don't see any possibility of that at all. If she killed that unfortunate young man it must have been an act of insane jealousy; that she appears to be reasonable and normal now means nothing. If she is an aggressive person—and we have every reason to believe that she is—she may become violent again, when the circumstances are right. She may have been jealous of the young man because he was making an impression on the girl. The girl is still alive. We don't want Mary van Krompen to kill the girl as well, do we?"

Grijpstra was nodding.

"You agree, adjutant?"

"I am afraid I do," Grijpstra said. "The girl will suspect Mary of having killed Tom Wernekink. She may say something to that effect."

"Yes," de Gier said.

The commissaris was still doing his gymnastic exercises. He stopped now and looked at his visitors. "Thank you for your time, gentlemen," he said softly.

4

IT WAS THE FOURTH TIME DE GIER PASSED THE HOUSE AND
he still hadn't found a parking place. The unmarked Volks-
wagen was a police vehicle, of course, and he didn't have
to worry about getting a ticket, but he did worry about the
huge truck behind him, hooting impatiently.

"Yes," de Gier muttered, "I'll get out of your way, but
where do I put the car?"

The truck driver honked his horn again. De Gier accelerated. "Walk," he said in a loud voice. "Walk! It'll be good
for you."

Houses crowded the dike on both sides and any free land
had been fenced in. He drove to the end of the dike where
the road widened and parked under a "No Parking" sign.
Then he walked back. The walk took ten minutes. He passed
Mary van Krompen's house and began to count. "Here," he

said and stopped on the narrow footway. The house looked in good repair, a two-storied cottage painted dark green.

"Cat with Boots On," de Gier muttered. It was all he knew. A friend of Thomas Wernekink. The only visitor ever seen in Wernekink's house. So far the people on the dike had been of very little help. Even Mary hadn't told them much, not even during the third interrogation. The commissaris would be talking to her again right now but she would probably be repeating herself: "No, I didn't kill him."

Evelien Dapper hadn't told them much either. This Cat with Boots On would be some strange type, a man who always dresses in corduroy suits. Unusual suits. Gold colored, or violet, or some other weird shade. Wears boots, high boots, very shiny. Long black hair and a heavy mustache. Big brown eyes. A large nose. Lives with his girlfriend, a beautiful woman. Mary claimed the Cat was in business; Evelien didn't know or care. And de Gier knew the Cat's age. Around forty years old, as old as de Gier himself.

"And there's something else I know," de Gier said as he pressed the bell again. "He isn't in." There was no nameplate on the door. "Pity Grijpstra isn't here," de Gier thought, but Grijpstra was in Rotterdam, checking up on Wernekink's background. Headquarters was short of detectives. The corpse in the canal and the corpse in the park had both proved to be baffling cases and the possibility of crime couldn't be ignored, so Geurts and Sietsema and even young Cardozo— the new detective who had been assigned to the "murder squad"—were ferreting about, sniffing for tracks and connections.

De Gier cursed. He had read the reports on the two corpses and felt certain there had been no crime. The dead girl in the park would be an ordinary heroin case, killed by her own needle. The old lady floating in the canal was sure to have fallen in. She had been full of alcohol. Perhaps she had been pushed but why push an old drunken woman who would fall into the canal by herself if left alone long enough? She had been well known in a number of cheap pubs. And the girl with the needle pricks on her arms was also known.

Maybe this Cat is mad, de Gier thought. Maybe he'll come charging out of the house firing an old muzzle loader. If he dresses like that he may be deranged in other ways too. And everybody who lives on this crazy dike knows I'm a policeman. They probably warned him off. I've been driving the VW to and fro for the last half hour and everybody knows the police use VW's; it's high time we changed our taste. They should give us Porsches like the state police use on the speedways, or Ferraris. A Ferrari would be just the thing to race around in. They are small and fast, and they look all right and...

The door opened. "Yes?" the beautiful woman asked.

Beautiful, de Gier thought. God shit almighty she is beautiful. That's all he thought. The definition was unavoidable. She really was beautiful.

"Morning, madam," de Gier said. "I am a policeman. Can I come in?"

"Of course," the woman said. "You don't have to be a policeman to come in. By all means come in—even if it's only for your own safety. That footway is dangerous. People are always being hurt by motorized bicycles here. These young men have no sense. They race around and if there's a car or something obstructing their way they take the footway. I hate them. Come in."

She walked ahead of him in the narrow corridor and de Gier kept on repeating his original thought but something had been added to it. He had noticed the size of the woman.

De Gier was a little over six feet tall but the woman was taller. Six-foot-three perhaps.

It doesn't matter, de Gier thought; the proportions are right. It doesn't matter at all. He noted the firm buttocks accentuated by her well-fitting slacks and the shapely bare feet. He also saw the long dark brown hair hanging down her back.

"In here," the woman said; "this is our best room. It has a view of the river. You are just in time for coffee. Have you come about the death of that poor man on the dike?"

"Yes, madam."

"My name is Ursula," the woman said. "Ursula Herkulanovna. I am Russian. You can call me Ursula. What's your name?"

"De Gier."

She pulled a face. The large sensuous mouth pouted. "Bah. I hate names starting with a G. You pronounce them so horribly, as if there were a live fly in your throat. What's your first name?"

"Rinus."

The mouth still sulked.

"You don't like 'Rinus' either?"

"No," she said.

"You can call me sergeant," de Gier said hopefully.

"Sergeant?" Ursula asked. "Is that all you are? My grandfather was a colonel of the Czar."

"That's all I am—sergeant," de Gier said. "Sergeant Rinus de Gier."

"Never mind," Ursula said. "You still get coffee, sergeant. I'll never get used to this country. Low ranks are important here I think. There was a man here the other day; he said he was a clerk, but he came from the Tax Department and he threatened to confiscate the house and the car and everything the Cat and I own because we hadn't paid tuppence halfpenny to some official or other. He was very nice too."

"The clerk?" de Gier asked.

"Yes. A big man. He said he rows boats on the river for fun. You do that as well, sergeant?"

"No," de Gier said firmly.

"But surely you go in for some sort of sport?"

"No," de Gier said. "All I do is feed my cat and water my plants on the balcony."

Ursula laughed, a full-throated laugh. She was standing very close to de Gier and suddenly she bent forward and brushed his cheek with her lips. "I like you, sergeant. You don't show off. This rowing man sat here for hours and told me all about himself. A champion rower. I couldn't get rid of him. He looked nice, with his wide shoulders, narrow hips and strong face, but he bored me to tears. The Cat was upset too when he came in and found this clown in the house. He gave him his pennies and showed him the door."

"Isn't the Cat in?" de Gier asked.

"No. As a matter of fact I am supposed to go fetch him. He is in town somewhere and hasn't got his car, but there is no hurry. Sit down and smoke a cigarette and look at the boats on the river; I'll get the coffee. I have some cake too. What sort of cake do you like?"

"Whipped cream and pineapple," de Gier said.

"That's what goes on top of the cake; I just have cake."

"No cake, please," de Gier said, and stared as Ursula slid out of the room. She slid, de Gier thought and lit a cigarette. His hand shook a little; he could feel the after effect in his spine of the brushing lips. She didn't walk, she slid, he mused. Girls do that on Grijpstra's TV but they always look ridiculous—this woman looks very elegant when she moves. And did you see her breasts?

He looked out the window without seeing the antique sailing craft tacking upstream. The boat looked most impressive carrying all her sails, mainsail, foresail and jib. De Gier liked boats; he could spend hours watching them, but he didn't see this boat even though it passed close by the windows.

Yes, he told himself, I saw her breasts. Men always go for breasts. Of course I saw them. And her shoulders. But everything is perfect about her. Her hands too.

He pushed his lips out and blew all the air out of his lungs. It was a trick the judo instructors had taught him in the police gymnasium. When you fall or get pushed suddenly or find yourself in an unexpected and difficult position, breathe out. Then breathe in slowly again. Shake your head. Start again. He shook his head. This, definitely, was a sudden and difficult position to be in. He hadn't expected Ursula.

Ursula, de Gier thought and frowned. He had known a girl called Ursula, a long time ago when he was still at school. A dumpy little thing with a faint mustache and pimples. A girl who always got top marks. He would have to get used to this new association. The other Ursula had been a powerful girl as well and he had disliked her wholeheartedly.

The breathing exercise cleared his brain and he now had an opportunity to study his surroundings. The room was well designed and well furnished. Stone tiles, white plaster walls, a modern oil painting showing two little boys shooting marbles in what seemed to be a desert. There were a lot of flowering plants—some of them delicate—that reminded him of pictures of a clearing in a tropical forest. Orchids.

He remembered that orchids require a lot of care. Perhaps Ursula cared for the plants, or would it be the mysterious Cat? He looked around for photographs but there weren't any. Strange, he thought, everybody displays photographs, with silver frames, on the piano. There was no piano either. The furniture was heavy, three chairs grouped around the window, large comfortable chairs with a profusion of cushions. A dining table had been pushed against the wall. He was admiring a subtle and intricately designed Persian rug that covered half the floor, when Ursula came back carrying a tray.

"Here," she said, "pineapple with whipped cream."

"I was only joking," de Gier said.

"You aren't going to eat it? I whipped the cream specially for you and opened a can."

"Sure, I'll eat it," de Gier said, and scratched his bottom. "Thanks a lot. Very nice of you."

"Hey," Ursula said.

"Pardon?"

"You're scratching your bottom," Ursula said. "Do you always do that? What a disgusting habit!"

De Gier stopped scratching and blushed. Ursula giggled. "You mustn't mind what I say. Go on, eat your cream. I'll watch you. I'm on a diet."

De Gier began to eat, closing his eyes with every spoonful and grunting to himself with delight. "Marvelous," he muttered. "Delicious. Absolutely delicious. This is the best cream I have ever eaten and the pineapple tastes as if it were picked an hour ago."

"Stop that," Ursula said, watching him carefully.

But de Gier didn't stop and when he was halfway through his plate Ursula screamed and pulled the dish out of his hands. "You're driving me crazy," she said and gobbled what he had left.

De Gier grinned.

"You are evil," Ursula said, opening her eyes until they glared from above the high cheekbones. "Can you imagine what I'll look like when I grow fat? I'm enormous already and with fat on my bones, horrible yellow grease, I'll be a pudding of flesh. Do you want me to change into a gigantic pudding? Do you?" She almost screamed the last words at him.

"No," de Gier said happily, "and you shouldn't worry about your size. You are big, of course, but you don't look bad."

She put the dish down with a clatter. "What's the matter with you?"

"Nothing. Why?"

"Don't look so innocent," Ursula said. "You are being pretty nasty you know. Men either flatter me or they run. You are doing neither. What do you want anyway?"

"I would like to meet your husband," de Gier said, "to ask him a few questions. We are investigating the death of Tom Wernekink and have been told that your husband used to see him now and then."

"Husband?"

"The Cat," de Gier said.

"The Cat isn't my husband. I live with him, or he lives with me. My husband is in Australia; he is a silly little man and I am divorcing him."

"Tell me," de Gier said, and sipped his coffee.

"Tell you what?"

"Anything. About your being Russian and about Australia and your grandfather being a Russian officer and how come you speak Dutch so well, and about the Cat, and about Tom Wernekink. Anything. I don't understand, you see."

"Ah," she said and stretched out on a chair, putting her bare feet on the table. "The police are curious. Or are *you* curious?"

"Both," de Gier said.

"All right. My father was born in Shanghai after my grandfather had escaped from the horrible communists. My father married my mother, who is Dutch. Then they had to escape from Shanghai because the horrible communists were coming again. We went to Australia, or rather they went for I wasn't born yet. Then I was born. I grew up in Australia and met the little man who married me. And then the Cat came on some business or other and told me about Amsterdam. It all sounded so romantic and I am half Dutch after all, so I took my passport and a suitcase and sneaked out of the house to follow the Cat. And here I am. I have been here for years now, five years I think."

"And Herkulanovna is your own name?"

"My father's name. I am still called Mrs. Graham, I suppose, but I am trying to forget the name. Soon I'll be divorced, I think."

"And then you'll marry the Cat."

She jumped up. "Never. I'll never marry again."

"You don't like the Cat?"

She sat down and finished the last bit of cream and pineapple. "Yes. I like him. But I play the flute; I want to travel and play the flute, and I don't want the Cat tagging along."

"Show me the flute," de Gier said.

"Why?"

"I play the flute too," de Gier said.

"Do you play well?"

"No. I play some baroque but usually I improvise with my colleague, Adjutant Grijpstra. He has a set of drums in our office; he bangs away and I put in a few trills here and there."

She laughed. "How lovely. Drums? Real drums?"

"A complete set. Somebody dumped it into our office, years ago now, and we never allowed it to be taken out again. Grijpstra used to play drums when he was a teenager and he started practicing again, very softly of course so as not to disturb the people in the rooms next door. Then I remembered that I used to play the flute; I found it again and now we play together."

"How very nice," Ursula said in a ladylike voice, "how very *very* nice. You must come play with me one evening. The Cat won't like it but we will send him away."

"Yes," de Gier said; "let's see your flute."

She produced a black leather box and de Gier took out the flute, assembling it carefully.

"Go on. Play," Ursula said.

"It's much bigger than mine," de Gier said, feeling his way on the instrument. The first note faltered but the second was much stronger.

"Can you read music?"

"Yes," de Gier said.

"Try this." She put a sheet of music on the table.

De Gier recognized the part. He shook his head. "Too intricate, especially on an instrument I don't know."

De Gier took out the small flute that he carried in his inside pocket. Ursula took the flute from his hands and held it in the palm of her hand.

"Beautiful," she said. "These small flutes are expensive; I wanted to buy one the other day but the Cat didn't have enough on him. He'll buy me one later, he said. Let's hear its sound."

De Gier blew a long piercing note and then began to play the music that he read from the sheet. He almost stopped when Ursula's flute joined in. The very first note was so round and full and perfect that he felt shy of his own piercing shrieks, but he looked up and saw the recognition in her eyes and bravely persisted, fighting the temptation to change his style. Soon his quivering song rested on an underground of flowing fluent sound until he felt as if he were a diving bird that flew above and dived through the quiet surface of Ursula's music. They had, by then, forgotten the written notes on the sheet and were playing something of their own, keeping it simple while feeling for each other's talent.

"Vivaldi would have liked that," Ursula said. "You know about Vivaldi?"

"A composer," de Gier said; "that's about all I know. Baroque. I have played some of his pieces."

"He was a priest," Ursula said, "a wild priest. He taught the nuns and he had red hair. Some of the nuns' children also had red hair."

De Gier grinned.

"Music is very much like sex, don't you think?" There was a light in Ursula's eyes and de Gier stepped back.

"Yes, yes," he said. "Pity my colleague Grijpstra isn't here. He could have joined in. Some of his drumming is very subtle now."

"Grijpstra," Ursula said. "I think we can do without him and his drums today. Anyway, we have to go. Are you ready?"

"Go where?"

"Don't you want to meet the Cat? I must pick him up and you can drive."

"My car is at the other side of the dike," de Gier said. "You'll have to wait a while for me to collect it."

"Nonsense, we can take my car; it's parked next to the house."

"But didn't you say I had to drive?"

"Yes," Ursula said. "You drive my car. I only got my license last week and I don't much like driving."

The car turned out to be a Morris Minor, brand-new and bright red. De Gier twisted himself behind the wheel and Ursula pushed the other chair as far back as it would go.

"Ursula, Ursula, where are you going?" piped a small voice. De Gier opened his door to see where the sound was coming from and discovered a child standing near the front wheel on his side.

"Who are you?" he asked the dirty little boy who kept on yelling, "Ursula," at the top of his voice.

"Darling," Ursula said and got out of the car. She picked the child up and cradled him in her arms. "My sweet, what have you been doing; you are full of mud and snot again."

"Yours?" de Gier asked.

"No. He belongs to the people next door. Isn't he a little darling? He isn't four years old yet but he is an absolute genius. Aren't you, sweet?" She kissed the child.

"Bah," de Gier said.

Ursula got back into the car and the child clambered over her lap and began to play with the gearshift. De Gier started the engine and pushed the gearshift into first. The child pulled it out of his hand.

"Put that child in the back, please," de Gier said in a strained voice, and Ursula picked the boy up. By the time the car joined the traffic on the dike the child was at the shift again, forcing de Gier to hold on to it. The child, finding that the lever wouldn't budge, began to fiddle with whatever he could so that the car's lights and blinkers were flashing on and off.

"Shit," de Gier said.

"Don't be miserable," Ursula said; "he's a little dear. I'll hold on to him. You just drive."

"Where are we going?"

She gave an address on the other side of the city and de Gier checked the dashboard. "We are almost out of petrol. Look at that red light going on and off—must be a warning light of some sort."

"Nonsense. I'm sure the Cat filled the tank yesterday; these indicators never work on new cars."

They ran out of petrol in the tunnel and de Gier sweated as the tunnel's warning lights went on. A siren began to howl and a salvage truck came screaming down.

"Out of petrol," de Gier said to the truck driver.

"Stupid, aren't you?" the driver said. "That'll cost you forty guilders. Pay in advance please."

De Gier showed his police identification.

The driver bent down and whispered into de Gier's ear. "Listen," he said, "you have your wife and child in the car so you are not on duty. We have been told that we should report cases like this. I haven't seen your card; pay, and I'll forget it."

"I am on duty," de Gier said fiercely.

The man sighed and brought out a notebook and a ballpoint. "Name, rank and police station," he said.

"De Gier, sergeant, Headquarters."

"Boy, oh boy," the driver said, "all that trouble for forty guilders. I'm glad I'm not in your shoes. You're sure you don't want to pay? If you haven't got any cash I'll take a check or any piece of paper and you can pay later."

De Gier shook his head.

"Right," the driver said, scowled and attached a hook to the front of the Morris. They were dumped at the parking lot at the end of the tunnel. The truck driver detached the hook and walked back to his truck.

"Hey," de Gier shouted, "I am out of petrol; don't leave me here. Tow me to the petrol station over there."

The man never turned around.

"He's stupid, isn't he?" the child said to Ursula.

"Hush."

"Why can't he drive? You can drive this car, can't you?"

"Hush."

"Do you have a jerrican in the car?" de Gier asked, fighting to keep his voice under control.

"No."

"I'll be back soon."

De Gier walked. The station was farther than he thought and when he got there, the attendants were busy and he had to wait.

"Yes?" an attendant asked finally.

"I am out of petrol," de Gier said. "Can you lend me a can and sell me five or six liters?"

"Mate," the attendant said. "Please! We have no cans and we're busy. There are three cars waiting for me now— this is peak hour."

"Please," de Gier said.

"Sorry."

"Look," de Gier said and put a hand on the man's shoulder, "look over there. See that small red car with the lady and child standing next to it? That's my car and my wife and my child. We are stuck. The child has to go home to eat. He's howling. You have to help me."

"I have a can without a handle," the man said.

"Anything."

"Let me serve those three cars first."

De Gier waited. The second car wanted oil as well. The third car wanted oil, its screen wiped and the pressure of the tires checked. The attendant got a big tip in advance and spent a full seven minutes. The can was an awkward size and de Gier had trouble carrying it. It was hot and his jacket stuck to his back. He carried the can on his shoulder and the petrol slopped out.

"You are slow, aren't you?" the child asked.

"Be nice to uncle," Ursula said. "He's helping us."

"He can't drive."

"I can't drive," de Gier said.

"Your father had a long walk, didn't he?" the attendant said to the child as they stopped to return the can and fill the tank.

"He is not my father," the child said. "He is my uncle and he can't drive."

The attendant raised an eyebrow at de Gier, who shrugged. "Would your wife like a pair of free sunglasses?" the attendant asked. "We are giving them away today. Every tenth car gets a pair."

"Wife?" Ursula asked.

"No thanks," de Gier said and looked at Ursula. "The bill came to twenty-five guilders."

"I didn't bring my bag," Ursula whispered.

De Gier paid.

The traffic was very thick and a number of accidents had clogged the city. They waited at lights that changed color without causing any movement in the interminable rows of cars, buses and trucks that had formed at the crossroads. It was getting hot in the car and the child complained. He wanted a drink and he wanted to go to the toilet. De Gier freed the Morris from the queue and parked the car on the sidewalk. He gave Ursula some money and she took the child to a café. A uniformed constable stopped and began to fill in a ticket. De Gier showed his identification.

"Are you on duty, sergeant?"

"Yes."

"Sure?"

"Yes."

Ursula came back with the child. As the constable opened the door for her, he bent down and whispered over to de Gier, "You are quite sure, aren't you, sergeant?"

"Yes."

"That wouldn't be your wife and child?"

"No."

"Suspects in a murder case?"

"Yes."

"We have been asked to write reports about things like this, sergeant."

"Do that."

"I won't," the constable said and wandered off.

De Gier was sweating. He was still sweating when they reached the speedway and were coasting toward the south. The child had fallen asleep on the back seat and Ursula's hand was resting on de Gier's thigh.

"Sergeant," Ursula's low voice said, "I am unhappy."

De Gier didn't answer. He tired to concentrate on the traffic and his hands, holding the diminutive steering wheel, were wet.

"Do you know why?"

He shook his head.

"The Cat is boring me. The house is getting smaller every day. I want to get out; I want to fly away. Where do you live, sergeant?"

"Not far away," de Gier said, pointing vaguely ahead.

"Let's go there."

"With the child?"

"We can give him a toy. He is a nice little boy."

"No, no," de Gier said.

Ursula looked out the window. She was talking to herself. "Another scared little man. Like the milkman last week. You asked him and he didn't dare. Scared little men can't do anything for you. You'll have to wait. One day it will come."

"What will come?" de Gier asked.

"Were you listening?"

"You were talking at the top of your voice."

"The boom-boom," Ursula said, "the great boom-boom orgasm. I have heard about it but I have never had it. The Cat is too busy; he's an adventurer, not a lover. I want a lover. You haven't got a ring on your hand; are you married, sergeant?"

"No," de Gier said.

"You have girls of course," Ursula said sadly.

"No," de Gier said, "it isn't that."

"Boys?"

"For God's sake," de Gier said.

"So?"

"The Cat," de Gier said. "You are living with the man, aren't you?"

"Are you frightened of the Cat?" Ursula asked. "You don't even know him. He isn't jealous. He's busy. Sometimes I don't see him for a week."

"No," de Gier said. The petrol on his shoulder had dried but the smell was still hovering in the car and he felt bilious. The child had begun to snore and some spittle was dribbling down his chin. Ursula had adjusted her hair and he had seen the wet spot under her armpit. The woman was still beautiful—he could see that—but all he wanted now was a bath and the company of his cat, Oliver, and a glass of iced coffee perhaps. No. The thought of coffee aggravated the sick feeling in his stomach. Just a bath, and Oliver stretched out next to him. The cat would have sense enough to be quiet. Ursula was still talking.

"Boom-boom orgasms. You think that's silly talk, don't you? You think I am a frustrated girl living in the body of a woman. Perhaps you are right. But surely I have a right..."

"Yes," de Gier said, "you have your rights. Here's the address." They had arrived at a large modern warehouse. The sign at the entrance said "Sharif Electric."

The Cat was waiting for them in the lobby. Ursula introduced the two men.

"De Gier. Municipal Police. Ursula asked me to drive her here. I have some questions to ask."

The Cat looked as he had been described by Evelien. He was smiling and shaking de Gier's hand.

"Diets is my name," the Cat said, "but call me Cat, everybody calls me Cat. I have to think of my real name sometimes."

"Listen," de Gier said, "I am running behind schedule and have to leave. Would it be convenient for you to come see me at Headquarters this afternoon at four-thirty?"

"Sure," the Cat said; "I'll be there. What is it about? Tom's death?"

"Yes," de Gier said.

"Poor fellow. I don't know if I can tell you anything but I'll help as much as I can. Tom was a friend of mine."

"Good. Good-bye, Ursula; thanks for the coffee and the ride."

"And the cream?" Ursula asked.

"And the cream."

"And the pineapple?" Ursula asked.

"And the pineapple."

"Goodbye, uncle," the child said.

De Gier left. He stopped a police car and asked them to drop him at a taxi stand. He took a taxi to the dike, collected the VW and drove home. He had an hour to wash and lie on his bed.

Oliver greeted him at the door by standing up against his leg. The cat's nails were out but his gesture was so slow and gentle that de Gier only felt a vague scratch. Oliver's eyes were half-closed and he was growling. De Gier scooped him up, turning him upside down, and the cat's face touched his cheek. The growl changed into a deep purr. Oliver stretched his front paw, spreading his toes, each toe ending in a long razor-sharp claw, and touched de Gier's nose with the furry underneath. "Careful," de Gier said and shook the cat. The paw stayed on his nose but the nails were only touching air.

"Oliver," de Gier said, "would you like a boom-boom orgasm?" The cat purred.

"You wouldn't know, would you, since I had you castrated? Remember? Fours years ago now? How you got your injection and you fell asleep and when you woke up the balls were gone and the little bag sewn up?"

The cat stopped purring, stretched and twisted himself free, landing on the floor with a soft thud.

"No, it didn't hurt," de Gier said. "You were sleepy, that was all. I'm sorry I had it done to you, believe me. Very sorry. A horrible thing. But you were tearing about the flat all the time and hanging on the curtains and yelling and yowling. I couldn't have kept you like that. Maybe I should never have bought you. Maybe you would have gone to people with a garden and trees and other cats, and birds to chase."

De Gier began to undress. "I'll take a shower, get the smell off my body. Petrol, bah. Petrol and sweat and car fumes and the fumes of Ursula and the stink of that child. Horrible child. Are you angry, Oliver, that you don't know about orgasms?" The cat rolled over on his back and squeaked.

"Can't you make a normal cat's noise? Or are you too extraordinary? Because you are Siamese? Because your grandfather came from the Far East? Go on, make a normal noise." Oliver squeaked again.

"Don't then. I'll have a shower; come with me and talk to me." The cat sat on the threshold and looked at de Gier standing under the shower. The hot water was hitting him in the neck and he was singing to himself. A song about Ursula and Ursula's beauty.

What would have happened, de Gier thought, if I had brought her home? Oliver would have murdered that horrible child for sure, but suppose the child hadn't come? Would she have stripped and raped me? Or would she have sunk on the bed and looked at me languorously? Shall I try it sometime? He imagined and got excited. The excitement annoyed him and he twisted the shower's dial so that the water suddenly changed into a whip of ice. He jumped out of reach of the whip but went back to it and shouted and jumped up and down. He twisted the tap and began to rub himself dry.

The cat snuggled next to him on the bed. There were thirty minutes to go; he set the alarm and fell asleep at once.

⫼⫼⫼ 5 ⫼⫼⫼

"So you are the Cat with Boots On," the commis-saris said. "We've heard a little about you. Just the way you dress and that you used to visit Tom Wernekink."

"Evelien Dapper told you, I suppose," the Cat said, "the girl who lives next door to Tom. I have spoken to her but I don't know her really."

The Cat was in the commissaris' office at Headquarters, sitting in the chair reserved for important visitors. Although Headquarters of the Amsterdam Municipal Police was a fairly modern building, the commissaris had managed to create a seventeenth-century atmosphere in the large high-ceilinged room. The antique furniture was his private prop-erty but the large Golden Age portraits decorating the walls belonged to the police. He had offered his visitor a cigar and the two men were puffing away, facing each other, with de Gier at a respectable distance, slouched in a chair in the corner, smoking a self-made cigarette. The Cat had arrived on time. He turned toward de Gier. "I hope Ursula didn't cause you any undue trouble? She is a strange woman. She could have driven the car herself; she has a license."

"I wasn't familiar with the car," de Gier said, "and the child didn't help much."

"The child!" the Cat said and laughed. "I gave him a clout on the ear and he was all right after that."

"Good."

"What's all this?" the commissaris asked.

"My car is being serviced," the Cat said, "and I asked Ursula, my girlfriend, to pick me up in town where I had some business to take care of. Your sergeant came to find me, and Ursula made him drive the car."

"And the child?"

"Not mine. Some nasty brat who lives on the dike. His parents don't look after him and he is always in the street. If he sees anyone he usually tries to go with them."

"Isn't he a nice child?"

"No," the Cat exclaimed, "he is a proper bastard with the brain of a full-grown genius. He learns a lot in the street. He's four years old now but I think he knows more than most children of fourteen. And the damned thing is that he is destructive. He breaks windows and takes hubcaps off cars and throws them into the river; he trips people up and if he can't do anything physical, he teases. Didn't he tease you, sergeant?"

"Yes."

"Yes?" the commissaris asked, amused. "And what did he do?"

"There was no petrol in the tank so we got stuck in the middle of the tunnel under the river. He told me I couldn't drive."

"Ah," the commissaris said. "There was a telephone call about that, I meant to tell you. The chief of the tunnel phoned to ask whether you were on duty today."

"I hope you told him I was," de Gier said sulkily.

"I did. What was the trouble?"

"They wouldn't believe me, thought that the Cat's girl-friend was my wife and the child our child."

"New regulations," the commissaris said. "Apparently somebody has been waving his police card around too often and there have been complaints to the chief constable; you didn't have to pay, did you?"

"No, sir."

"Just as I thought," the Cat said sadly, "so she did get you into trouble. She didn't have any money I'm sure and made you pay for the petrol. How much was it, sergeant?"

"Twenty-five."

The Cat brought out a fat wallet and peeled a note out of one of its compartments.

"What is your business, Mr. Cat?" the commissaris asked.

"Call me Cat, commissaris, everybody does." The Cat put the wallet back and turned the ends of his large mustache. "I am a buyer and seller. Odd lots mostly, anything people want to get rid of. I have a warehouse in town that is full of carpet tiles right now—bought them from Sharif Electric where the sergeant found me today. They had an exhibition and had to buy a few square miles of carpet but now it's of no use to them so they sold it to me."

"For cash?"

"Always for cash. It's the only way to buy. Nobody resists bank notes. The wallet and this costume are tricks of the trade."

"Costume?"

"Yes," the Cat said. "I know I dress crazy but it gives

me the right image. Nobody forgets me, once they have seen me. I give them my card with my photograph, address and phone number, and if there's anything to sell I usually get first chance. I joke and wave the wallet about and I get the goods."

"You look funny," the commissaris said, "but you don't look like a hippie or a provo or a bird-of-protest."

"No. I have no quarrel with the world. The world is wrong, of course; anybody who can see and think knows it is wrong. The wrong place and we do the wrong thing. But I don't mind. I'm not a fighter; I'm a buyer and seller. I make a profit and I spend some of it."

"Who do you sell to?"

"People come to me. The merchants from the street markets, and the secondhand shops, and the discount stores. I have a lady in the warehouse and she knows the prices. Usually I'm there as well, if I'm not on holiday. I often go away—I'll go anywhere and usually I manage to buy there as well. The world is full of merchandise; it's amazing it's still turning with all that weight attached to it."

"And Ursula is your girlfriend?"

The Cat nodded. "Yes. I found her in Australia and she wanted to come to Amsterdam; she is half-Dutch, half-Russian."

"And she is beautiful," de Gier said.

The Cat smiled. "She is, isn't she? But she is crazy too. Did she try to make you?"

De Gier looked silly and the commissaris smiled.

"I hope she didn't succeed, de Gier," the commissaris said.

"No, sir."

"There's a good fellow."

"She always says she is going to leave me," the Cat said,

"but she hasn't so far. She is free to do as she likes. I don't collect anything. My house is like my warehouse: its contents come and go."

"You want to get rid of her?" de Gier asked.

"No. If she stays, she stays. I like her, and she isn't a useless type. She's a good musician and she sometimes plays in town. Maybe she'll be invited to travel and then, perhaps, she'll go. She needs to meet other men, men who can handle her. Maybe you could handle her." He looked at de Gier as if he was weighing him. De Gier didn't feel comfortable, the large brown eyes seemed to be piercing through his skull. The man's personality was definitely powerful. The Cat looked majestic sitting straight up now, the wide shoulders sloping slightly, the massive head erect with its mane of hair, the fierce nose pointed at de Gier's forehead. And he wasn't dressed so funny after all. The velvet gold-colored suit sat very well on the large body and the boots were elegant and shiny. De Gier noticed a thick, gold earring on the Cat's left earlobe. A few hundred years back in time and the Cat would have been easy to place: a gentleman-pirate or highwayman, sporting a sword with a jeweled handle. A courageous man, a gallant man.

An immoral man, the commissaris was thinking. A profiteer, but perhaps with a code of honor. Not a man who would betray a friend, or his own people, to an enemy, but still . . . "Do you have an officially registered business, Mr. Cat?" the commissaris asked.

The Cat took his eyes off de Gier and fixed them on the commissaris; they were pleasant now and the voice drawled. "Yes, sir. Diets Trading Company, registered since 1945. My father started the business; he dealt in hair creams and wigs and combs—things like that. I still have a small trade in that line but my talent is different: I like buying anything that looks cheap."

"Tom Wernekink," the commissaris said. "We can have some coffee while you tell us about your friend. De Gier, you can pour the coffee; it's on the tray over there."

"Just a friend," the Cat said in the same drawling voice. "I saw him arrive on the dike and helped to unload the furniture. He interested me. We drank some beer after we had shifted the lot into his house and I kept coming back. He was a strange man, you know. I am really sorry they got him; I like strange people; there aren't too many around, not even in Amsterdam, which is the lunatic asylum of Holland."

"*They* got him?" the commissaris asked.

The Cat shrugged. "Somebody did, didn't he? Or she? Didn't you lock that van Krompen woman up? She hasn't confessed, has she, or I wouldn't be here now."

"You don't think she did it?"

"I don't know. According to the newspaper, Tom was shot between the eyes from a distance. Mary is a crack shot, so she could have done it. The people on the dike don't think so. They want her back by the way; she's popular. We had a street party some months ago and she organized it all. I think she has helped a few people who needed something. Yes, they want her back. They have been sending things to the police station, cakes and newspapers and cigarettes. You let them through, didn't you?"

"Certainly," the commissaris said, "but it wasn't necessary; we're looking after her. But it is nice to have friends, of course; she appreciates the gifts."

"Are you any good with a gun, Cat?" de Gier asked.

"No," the Cat grinned, or rather, showed his teeth. The thick beard separated from the mustache and there was a white gleaming line. The Cat looked ferocious for a few seconds, like a tiger crouching under a tree, not meaning to attack but asserting its presence.

"No," the Cat said, "I wasn't even in the army. There is something wrong with my left eye and I have to wear glasses when I drive or read. The eyes don't focus properly, I believe. The only time I ever handled a firearm was in Australia when I shot at clay pigeons with a shotgun; I didn't hit them."

"Tell me more about Tom Wernekink," the commissaris said, pushing a cup of coffee toward the Cat. "Help yourself to sugar and milk."

The Cat sipped his coffee and smacked his lips. "Not much to tell. Tom never said more than he had to. He came from Rotterdam. He'd worked in an office over there, silly work, filling in forms for export orders. I have to do that too at times—drives you crazy—every country is different and if you make a slight mistake you get the lot back and have to start all over again. Officials hate businessmen; it's the old story. Jealousy."

"Yes," said the commissaris.

"Sorry. You are an official too, I forgot. But the police are different; they have a sense of adventure too. I didn't mean the police. Tom Wernekink. Yes. His father died and left him a lot of money and all that furniture and paintings and stuff. I think he planned never to work again. I saw him in the evening once; it was a mistake. He just sat and watched TV and drank beer. It was better during the day, for he would be in his garden. We used to sit under that big chestnut tree and drink tea and talk; he didn't drink alcohol during the day."

"A man without ambition," the commissaris said.

The Cat got up, stretched and sat down again. "Yes, no

ambition. Worse perhaps. I think he suffered. A very morose man, not the sort of man who complains all day. Tom had passed that stage. He wanted nothing to do with anything; he thought life was absolutely ridiculous, absurd. A joke. A bad joke."

"Don't you think the same?"

"Yes, but I laugh a lot; Tom didn't laugh. I told him to use some of his money to travel and he went to England a couple of times but I don't think he enjoyed the trips. He didn't like leaving his garden. He fished but when he caught anything he would throw it back. He caught a big pike once—gave him a good fight—but the pike is back in the river; he wouldn't even show it to boast. I happened to see him catch it or I would never have known. If anyone catches a big fish on the dike there is a party, but Tom didn't want anybody around him."

"But he watched TV?"

"Not really. He saw objects and shapes move but I don't think he knew what was going on. He didn't care."

"And you don't know whether he had enemies?"

"No enemies," the Cat said, "I am sure of it. Who would want to harm him? Nobody even knew him except me, and perhaps the girl next door, Evelien."

"What about her?"

The Cat made a wide gesture. "Just a girl. Nice girl. Pretty girl. She liked him, or loved him, or I don't-know-whated him. Wanted to have him, I think. Women always want to have things, and keep them."

"Ursula," de Gier said suddenly.

The Cat turned round and de Gier felt the impact of the large brown eyes again. "Yes, sergeant, Ursula is an exception, but she is sick; she is under psychiatric treatment. Did she tell you?"

"No."

The Cat laughed. "Don't worry; she isn't dangerous. She switches off sometimes and sits and stares and doesn't function. I have to feed and bathe her; it's a job I tell you, for she is a big woman. The psychiatrist is helping but it takes time. She is much better now. She wants more out of life than life is prepared to give just now. She has to grow up and create something that will hold wisdom; so far she is still a foolish little girl."

"She plays the flute very well," de Gier said.

"Did she play for you?"

"We played together."

The Cat jumped up and clapped his hands. "Boy," he shouted, "I would like to hear that. Crazy Russian Ursula playing with a police sergeant. What did you play?"

"Something we made up."

"Better and better. Promise me you'll come one evening and play with her. What do *you* play?"

De Gier took the flute out of his inside pocket and showed it to the Cat, who treated the instrument with respect.

"Nice flute. They cost a lot of money—nine hundred I think. I wanted to buy one for her but I didn't have that much cash on me. Isn't the sound rather shrill?"

"Very," the commissaris said. "If he plays in his office I can hear him, and his office is a long way from mine."

The Cat was shaking his head.

The commissaris smiled.

"Not a bad day today," the Cat said. "I'm discovering things. So the police are a little crazy too, now what? It's spreading. We are not alone anymore."

"We?"

"I am not the only Cat," he said; "there are others. Sometimes we meet."

"Well," the commissaris said, "leave us one of your visiting cards and I think we're through for today. We won't detain you any longer; you must be a busy man. If we need you again we'll telephone."

"So?" the commissaris asked de Gier.

De Gier didn't answer.

"No conclusions? No combinations? Suspicions?"

"Why?" de Gier asked, "would a man as mad as the March Hare and the Mad Hatter combined ever kill a harmless recluse like Tom Wernekink. Or are we misinformed about Tom?"

"It all fits in so far," the commissaris said, rubbing his legs.

"I saw the house, you saw the house. We both saw the body. If Tom was engaged in any activity apart from gardening, a bit of pike catching and the beer and TV combination, we would have found indications of it, but there was nothing there. The man was obviously rotting away quietly and not even the garden was helping him much. Aggression is always connected with desire. He didn't want anything, did he? So why would anyone else want anything from him?"

"He was rich," de Gier said.

"Yes, but the killer didn't take anything. The money was still in his wallet."

"Perhaps a painting," de Gier said, "a Vermeer or a Rembrandt. There was such a lot of stuff in the house, we couldn't see if there was anything missing."

The commissaris scratched his thin hair. "Yes. Perhaps. But I saw the paintings on the wall and they were family portraits. Two hundred years old perhaps and worth something but nothing much, a few thousand guilders. And the walls were covered with paintings. If he had owned a really valuable work of art he would have hung it with the others. Or not?"

"I don't know, sir; he wasn't a normal man. He might have put it against a wall and the murderer took it."

The commissaris thumped the table. "Why didn't anyone *see* the murderer? That dike is always full of people. They should notice a stranger."

"They knew the murderer and are trying to protect him," de Gier said.

"Could be. But we have the approximate time of death. About eleven o'clock in the evening the doctor said, with a margin of two hours each way. They may be all drunk or asleep by that time."

De Gier cleared his throat. "Nasty case, sir."

"No, no, don't say that. Nasty for Mary van Krompen perhaps; I am sorry for the lady. She sits and says 'no' all the time and is uncomfortable. I wish I could let her go."

"Can't you?"

"The public prosecutor and the judge aren't in favor of the idea yet. The judge talked to her for a long time and isn't convinced at all, by the way."

"Are you?"

"No," the commissaris said, "and if this goes on for another few days I am going to throw my weight about and let her go."

"Shouldn't we warn the girl, Evelien I mean?"

"Even if she is in love with that girl she won't kill her," the commissaris said.

"We have been wrong before," de Gier said.

The commissaris was quiet for a long time and de Gier walked toward the door. "I am going home, sir."

The commissaris waved. De Gier's remark hadn't really registered.

"Did Grijpstra phone in?"

"What?"

"Grijpstra, sir; did he phone in?"

"Ah, yes. Nothing special. He found a friend of Tom's, a former neighbor, a cripple I think he said. Confirmed everything we found out so far. No contradictions. I told him to see me in the morning; he was phoning from Rotterdam railway station."

"Good night, sir," de Gier said and closed the door behind him.

⦚⦚⦚ 6 ⦚⦚⦚

"IT HAS NOTHING TO DO WITH ME," ADJUTANT GRIJPSTRA thought. He felt peaceful. The streetcar that was taking him that morning at eleven to the Rotterdam suburb of Kralingen was old and he might have been uncomfortable on his straight wooden seat, but instead a warm glow of contentment had spread itself through his ample body. The little old lady sitting opposite him approved of this solid gentleman, who was displaying such a warm and pleasant interest in the view outside the streetcar window.

"Nothing to do with me at all," Grijpstra thought again as he saw a bicycle go through a red light. In Amsterdam he would have been upset. He would have done nothing about the offense—a plainclothes detective is by nature secretive and doesn't show his hand unless he absolutely has to. But he would have been irritated. Rotterdam, to Grijpstra, was a totally foreign world. He had stared at the wide avenues and modern towering square buildings and had been mildly impressed, in the way he had been impressed during his last holiday when his youngest son had dragged him by the hand to study an ant's nest. Ants, Grijpstra thought, were diligent and intelligent animals. He didn't care about ants, though. There might be, as far as Grijpstra was concerned, no ants at all in the world. But there are. And ants, who live in groups, have to have laws. And laws will be broken. And there will be ants, dressed in blue uniforms and caps, who care about the broken laws.

Grijpstra saw a police car, a large white van marked with red shiny stripes and the word POLITIE in clear letters, following the unsuspecting cyclist. He saw the cyclist stop when the van passed him and spoke to him through its loudspeaker. He approved but he didn't feel the fierce joy that a similar incident would have caused had he been in his own familiar surroundings.

The little old lady stared at the man sitting so close to her and wished he were her son. She noted the blue suit with its thin delicate stripes. She also noted that the suit needed ironing. She saw the white shirt and the gray tie, the heavy square head with the bristling mustache and the light blue kindly eyes. Nice man, the lady thought and wondered what he did for a living. Business, she thought vaguely, but businessmen don't ride the streetcars anymore. Shopkeeper, she finally decided.

Grijpstra sighed. It was a sigh of pleasure. The streetcar had turned a corner and was now following the edge of a park. The tram rattled across a bridge and Grijpstra unfolded the map he had bought at the station. The suburb was getting closer. He still felt detached and it took some effort to remember what he was supposed to do.

Wernekink, Grijpstra thought and nodded to himself. He

had already done something about Wernekink that morning, without reaching any result. He had talked and listened to a man whose name he couldn't remember now but which he had written down in his notebook to use, in due course, in his report. A man who had once been Tom Wernekink's boss. The man hadn't been able to tell him anything new. The interview had been mere routine, without any interest on either side. The address of the firm that had employed Wernekink more than a year ago had been given to him by the Rotterdam police during the previous day in answer to a telephone call. He had found the office easily enough and had been led to a man who presided over a battery of clerks from a raised vantage point where, protected by glass walls, he could see exactly what was happening around him.

Yes, Wernekink had worked there for several years. No, he knew nothing about his private life. Tom Wernekink had arrived and left on time, hadn't been ill very often, and had done his job reasonably well.

Had there been anything at all that he remembered about Wernekink, the clerk who filled in forms? Yes. Wernekink never went to the canteen where the employees could buy a simple meal at ten percent above cost price. He ate at his desk. Brought half a loaf of brown, a jar of margarine and a jar of jam. Cut his bread, spread it on the desk, buttered it, spread jam on it, and ate it. He drank tea from a thermos flask. Then he read the paper. After the paper he worked again, as the clerks filed back to their desks.

"I didn't like it," the chief clerk said and shook his head, "didn't like it at all. The firm gives us a good canteen and proper food, and the chaps sit there and talk to each other and play cards. It's unhealthy to sit by yourself, asocial in a way. Don't you think?"

"Yes," Grijpstra said.

"And I didn't like the mess he made on his desk. All that margarine and jam. I spoke to him about it, told him that he might muck up his forms. But he still refused to go to the canteen, and there is no rule about it."

"So you let him get away with it," Grijpstra said, clearly indicating by his facial expression that Wernekink shouldn't have got away with it.

The man spread his hands. "What could I do?"

"Nothing," Grijpstra agreed.

"And now he's got himself killed, has he? Did he get himself a job in Amsterdam?"

"No."

"Laziness," the man said. "Drink, women. The free life. It's bad for them. We used to have a clerk here who rode a motorcycle, one of those big heavy ones. Would come in all dressed up in leather overalls and a helmet. You know the type—flirt with the girls and drink and have it all his own way. No, no."

"What happened to him?" Grijpstra asked.

"Got himself killed, in Persia or Turkey or somewhere. On holiday he was." The man looked pleased.

"It's the irregular life," Grijpstra said. "Looks all right but they can't do it."

"Exactly," the man said and meant to open up and tell the adjutant a long story that would explain and justify his simple but interesting philosophy of life. But the story never came. There had been something about the adjutant's face that changed and killed the chief clerk's intention. A twinkle in the pale blue eyes and a quiver of the cheeks.

Grijpstra read the name of the street the tram was crossing and put a thick finger on the map. Next stop he would have to get off. He pressed his left arm against his body and felt the bulge made by his notebook, which he kept in his wallet.

Then he pressed his right elbow against his hip and felt the bulge of his pistol. He folded the map and got up, nodding to the little old lady who smiled at him.

There were villas around him—large villas—mansions with huge parklike gardens, driveways, trees and lawns set off with bushes and clusters of high-growing pampa grass bending in the fresh breeze that tempered the heat of this summer day. Grijpstra studied the splendor of his surroundings and tried to work out what the occupants of this corner of heaven would have to be earning. He arrived at a large round figure. Then he tried to work out what they would have to be earning if they declared their true income. The figure doubled. He shook his head in surprise. But the houses, the driveways, the lawns were still there. And the expensive cars, which would be second cars given to wives to do their shopping, visit each other and perhaps take the children to school. He thought of his own house and Mrs. Grijpstra and the paint peeling off the ceiling of his small bathroom. The bathroom hadn't been there when he rented the house fifteen years ago and it had cost him a year's savings. These houses would have several bathrooms, all tiled.

He kept on walking, checking the house numbers on the way, still feeling peaceful. He found the number he was looking for and turned into a narrow gravel path. At the end of the path he had a choice between two houses, both small compared to the villas he had just been admiring. There were no numbers on the gates, so he chose one, walked up the path and rang the bell.

"I'm here," a voice said from the garden. He turned and saw a woman in an invalid chair. "What can I do for you?" She was wheeling herself toward him. He bowed down to her, shading his eyes from the sun.

"Morning, madam. I am a police detective from Amsterdam; I'm looking for the house where Mr. Wernekink used to live. Is this it?"

"No," the woman said, "it's the house next door but the people who live there are on holiday. Can I help you perhaps."

"Yes," Grijpstra said. "Perhaps you can."

"Come sit with me in the garden," the woman said and turned her wheelchair around.

When he left the garden it was three hours later and he had eaten a good lunch. The soft voice of the crippled woman was still somewhere inside his skull, vitalizing the various parts of his brain. There had also been the peace of the garden, protected by a good hundred meters of distance from the traffic of the main road. It was almost as quiet as a glade in a vast forest. Several thrushes and a pair of small dark-headed songbirds had been close to the crippled woman and himself while they sat and talked and ate a meal of fried eggs, fresh bread and a salad. She had prepared the meal in her old-fashioned but well-organized kitchen, wheeling around in her chair but making the minimal number of movements, for she knew exactly where everything was and seemed as efficient as a highly trained nurse during an intricate operation. He had carried the tray out and they had eaten in the shadow of an oak with the birds hopping about eating bits off the table. One of the songbirds had rested on his arm for a while, looking at him with bright little eyes, moving its head and occasionally lifting a wing to keep its balance. He still felt pity for the crippled woman and the memory of her grotesque and distorted body hurt him. She had, she told him, been struck by polio when she was still very young and the treatment had come too late.

Her chest was pushed up to her chin, one shoulder was raised as high as her ear and one leg was so twisted it was useless—only a weight to be dragged along—and the other was too short. He also admired the woman whose brain was clear and whose voice could understand and explain, but best of all he had liked the sound of her voice, which was like the sound of a Chinese flute. He couldn't remember now that he had ever heard a Chinese flute but he had a picture of a young girl playing one on a balcony that overlooked a rock garden and a pond surrounded by shrubs. The picture, part of a calendar that hung in the police canteen, had thrilled him so much he had taken it home when the month was up. He kept it in his desk at home in the same file with his insurance policy and police diplomas.

The crippled woman remembered Tom Wernekink well: the boy who lived next door with his old father, a retired businessman who read the newspaper and watched football on TV. Tom had come to talk to her and he often helped her around the house; they had tea and coffee together, under the same oak and with the same thrushes and songbirds.

"He talked to you?" Grijpstra asked, for he was under the impression that the corpse that had grinned at him a few days before had never talked to anyone. But she assured him that Tom did talk and that he was intelligent and able to communicate, even if he seemed to have no friends and no one ever came to visit him or his old father. But she also told him about Tom's negativity and his vegetative way of life. She pointed at a dead tree, lying in the garden next door. It had been Tom's seat and she had seen him there, immobile, for hours on end. Once it was raining and she tapped her window; Tom looked up and went indoors, soaked to the skin.

"Yes," Grijpstra said and began to get up, looking for

words to thank her for the lunch and the information he had
him solicited. She asked him to wait and wheeled her chair
indoors, up the special ramp that a carpenter had built so
that she would be able to get in and out easily. She came
back with a letter that Grijpstra promised to return. He read
the letter on his way back to the station in the same old
streetcar that had taken him to Kralingen earlier in the day.

Dear Liza,
How are you? How is the weather? And the birds, and the oak
tree? Did that stuff work that I gave you to keep the mosquitoes
away? I am sure Father didn't remember to water the laburnum;
give him a shout when you see him, will you? I have never
had laburnum before and the instructions say that it needs plenty
of moisture. I put the seeds in the ground near my dead tree.
If they come up they should grow all over the tree and their
flowers will hang down. There are three different colors: red,
orange and yellow. Perhaps I should have had yellow only.
This way the tree may look like the box top of some cheap
brand of horrible chocolates, but I can always snip off the
wrong flowers. I am a gardener after all, not a lover of nature.
To hell with nature. It doesn't care about us, so why should
we care about it? All this modern rubbish about pollution makes
me laugh; why are we so concerned all of a sudden?
   Let the sea get full of oil and the rivers full of boiling soapy
suds, I don't care. I only care about the garden and the dead
tree. If they take that away as well, I'll find another spot. And
if everything is mucked up, I'll grow a few mini plants in an
aquarium. Ah, I am being negative again; you don't like that
I remember. Sorry. It's the way I am. But it's true that you
have often cheered me up, for which I send you my respectful
thanks. It's nice to live in a different atmosphere sometimes.
I like you, Liza, and you are about the only person I like. I
don't like Father, the silly old buzzard, although he amuses
me at times, especially when his club loses. You should see
him stomp about the house.
   This holiday is drawing toward its end and good riddance
to it. I am in Cassis-sur-Mer as you can see by the postmark.
I shouldn't be here but it seems that I am always in a place

where I shouldn't be. I certainly shouldn't be in that silly office where I fill in the forms, but I have to return to it, so why grumble? And this Cassis-sur-Mer isn't the worst place on earth. The tourists haven't found it yet. I only found it because the brand-new car that Karel K. bought chose this convenient spot to break down completely. Something with the gearbox, I understand. Karel is in Marseilles; he had the car dragged there—it cost him a fortune—and it sits in a garage. He has taken a room in a hotel and goes to annoy the garage owner every day. A new gearbox has arrived and is being installed. I don't like Marseilles; it's a big city like any other although not quite as depressing as Rotterdam. I have begged him to let me stay here, in this little fishing port. At least I am close to the sea. Sometimes I take the bus to Marseilles and drink with Karel on a terrace. We drink Pernod, which hits you like a mule after a while, and watch the whores in the street. We make bets about whether or not they'll manage to catch a particular customer. I usually lose, for Karel is a good psychologist. And then, when we are drunk, we go to see a film. We only see French films and it's very enjoyable to make up your own story, fitting in the characters who shuffle or glide about the screen. I was so drunk the other day that I saw double and then it was even better. Two beautiful men kissing—or hitting; they hit each other a lot in these films—two beautiful women in two cars. I am glad I never bothered to learn French; we had it at school of course, seven hours a week, but the teacher was such an unbelievable clod that I refused to listen to him. And yet I passed the exam. Oh, life is full of miracles.

In spite of everything I am doing wrong I still seem to be picking up the language now. I caught myself thinking in French yesterday, not just a few words but complete sentences; I was even conjugating the verbs properly. The first French I read here was on the label of the Pernod bottle and I looked up the words I didn't know in Karel's dictionary.

Karel is a very pleasant chap, you know. Fancy that I have worked at the desk next to him for more than a year and I never knew that it would be such fun drinking Pernod with him. He is a bit like me, I think, poor fellow. But he is weaker, so he will survive. He was saying that he will probably get married, rent a flat and have children. He doesn't really want to but life is too strong he says; it's got him by the scruff of the neck and is shaking him. They'll take photographs at his wedding and they'll paste them in an album that he'll show to his friends and relations. Oh, poor gentle Karel. But who am I to sneer at him? Perhaps I want the same thing, although I doubt it. I really doubt it, Liza. And I doubt whether he wants all this family life and happiness and coziness and good cheer. Does anybody want it? Once the human animal was a hunter, lived in the forests and had a good time. Life was short. I read somewhere that the skeletons found in a grave a million years old all belonged to young people. There wasn't a skeleton to be found that had held a life older than twenty-five years. They ran about and had their adventures, and then a bear caught them, or the flu, or the plague, or the jealous lover. They had their skulls crushed when the fun was still on. And now we build concrete boxes and look at two-dimensional pictures that move, and we have an early night four times a week. It can't be right.

The biggest riddle—to me—is that I am sometimes quite happy. Two weeks ago, for instance. The chief clerk, a secondhand clown who you must never meet, brought me a whole heap of forms to be filled in and I was actually grateful. Can you imagine, dear Liza? I was *grateful*. The forms were some new model and I was looking forward to filling them in. Poor crazy me.

I had an adventure yesterday. I was walking about on the beach looking for a woman I'd met the night before—a nice woman with a nice figure. She had been alone and I had said something about the moon and the sea. I'd had a flask of cognac with me. She'd had a sip and I'd had a sip and it all ended the way I had wanted it to end. She hadn't seemed to be very enthusiastic but she had made the right movements and what more does a tourist want? Love in the moonlight on a deserted beach, heigh-ho and a bottle of Yo. I thought she might be on the beach again but that was silly of me, of course, for she had told me she was a nurse and would be on duty during the day. Anyway, I was ambling about when I saw a sand hill, a very steep hill and I climbed it to enjoy the view of the sea. The view was fine and I fell asleep. When I awoke I had moved to the edge of the hill; suddenly I felt myself rolling down. I didn't think it was so bad at first, but then I saw that I was heading for some sharp rocks and that I was actually *in danger of losing my life.* And I was frightened. I didn't want to lose my life. I, Tom Wernekink, wanted to live. Wasn't that a surprise? I managed to live, as you can see, for this isn't a letter from the Other Side, conveyed to you through the good offices of Madame Raqama, who will go into a trance at the drop of a hat and a twenty-five guilder note. I, your friend Tom, am writing the letter in my own spidery, illegible and unbalanced handwriting.

But it made me think. It destroyed my daydream of the Ideal Suicide. Karel and I worked it out the other day, plunging through a bottle and a half of Pernod. It was a complicated daydream but not quite impossible, I think. I'll try to describe it to you.

1) I study the currents and the times of high and low tide.
2) I buy three bottles of sleeping pills—no reason to be stingy—and a large bottle of the very best cognac.
3) I wait for the moon to be full; suicide is an act of lunacy and the first four letters of the word LUNA name our old friend, the round, mysterious, gently frightening body that rules the night.
4) I go to the beach.
5) I swim—holding on to the cognac bottle and the pills somehow—to a rock; the rock actually exists and it's about two miles from the shore here.
6) I manage to reach the rock and clamber on top of it; I sit down and sing my one and favorite song. I can't tell you the words of the song since it is a magic song and the words are mine alone. I'm sorry, Liza, but that's the way it is: every man must have at least one secret, mine is the song.
7) While I sing I watch the moon—obvious, of course, but I am giving you the complete recipe.
8) I swallow all the sleeping pills and drink the cognac. The bottle isn't full anymore, for I have already drunk some before swimming out.
9) I throw the bottles into the sea, stretch out and fall asleep.
10) The tide changes. A wave carries me off the rock and in the direction of the horizon.
11) The current takes over and I am moving at some speed.
12) I die.

13) The sharks come and eat me, bite-tear-swallow-gulp.

A nice clean death, don't you think? No rubbish, no nothing. I won't leave a farewell note. Tom Wernekink has joined the great beyond.

But I won't do it. What a pity. First I thought I wouldn't do it because it would be too much trouble. Working out the tides and the current and all that. But if I can fill in complicated export forms, I can make a few simple calculations, can't I? No, there's another reason. It's you, Liza. I admire you. If you can live I can. I am damned if I know why I should live but I'll go on. Still, I hope I won't live too long. I've really had enough of it. The angel should come and fetch me. I wonder what the angel of death will look like in Holland. He has to conform to the environment, of course. You know what I think? I think he will wear a dark suit, pointed shoes, and a dark tie. And he'll kill me with a pistol. It'll be late at night and he will call me, and when I come he will kill me. In a respectful manner, for angels are polite. They are very evolved and our reasoning and wishing and daydreaming and general silliness makes them smile. But when we really want them to come, they will come. Such is the law.

Enough of this. I can imagine you clearly. You are under the oak tree, reading this through that extraordinary pair of glasses you have. I must rush; the bus will be leaving in a few minutes and Karel can't drink without me. We have our responsibilities. Don't forget to tell Father to water the laburnum and give my love to the birds, the milkman, the postman and the mayor. Good day, dear Liza; see you soon.

The letter wasn't signed. Grijpstra folded the letter carefully and slid it into his side pocket. The commissaris would be interested, and de Gier, of course. He was interested himself. He sighed, but this time the sigh was sad. But he cheered up again. He wouldn't be at home for dinner. He would phone from the station and have a meal in the old city of Amsterdam, by himself, in a cheap Chinese restaurant. Then he would walk home and go to bed.

* * *

In the train, just before he fell asleep, a last thought flitted through his mind. "Catch the angel." He promised himself that he would. They would solve the case. It was a strange case but they had had strange cases before. The commissaris would solve it, de Gier would solve it, he would solve it. But they hadn't solved it yet.

⫻⫻⫻⫻ 7 ⫻⫻⫻⫻

GRIJPSTRA SLEPT QUIETLY AND IN HIS SLEEP THE BRIGHT-
eyed songbird was with him again. De Gier slept but kept
on turning, and Oliver jumped up everytime his master
turned and patiently found a new place to curl up in. De
Gier dreamed about Ursula whom he was following through
endless corridors. The commissaris didn't sleep. The pain
had awakened him earlier than usual that morning and he
was sitting in his study with a cup of very strong coffee and
a small cigar. He had opened the doors to the garden and
was observing the small turtle that lived in a wooden box
under the rhododendron bushes. The turtle was rowing itself
through the high grass on his way to a few lettuce leaves
that the commissaris had put on the threshold of his study.
The commissaris had no acquaintances and few friends, and
of his friends only the public prosecutor and the turtle knew
how to be with him in silence. The commissaris sipped his

coffee and the turtle plowed on in the clear light of the early morning.

The motorcycle and its sidecar glided through the clear light of the early morning. It wasn't yet six o'clock and both the constable, riding the silent BMW, and the sergeant, who was sitting on the edge of the sidecar, were dog-tired. They had taken part in a large exercise about sixty kilometers north of Amsterdam and all they wanted to do now was to park the cycle and sidecar in the large traffic police garage and catch a tram home. There they would grunt at their wives and go straight to bed and sleep for at least ten hours. The thought that they would have two consecutive days off was keeping them within the bounds of sanity and the constable was riding at exactly fifty kilometers per hour, in spite of the absence of all other traffic. The sergeant was staring straight ahead. He tried to forget the endless repetitions of the night. They had been doing anti-riot practice with a complete team of a dozen motorcycles, twenty horsemen and a hundred constables on foot, and cadets from the police schools of The Hague and Amsterdam. They had raced up and down through the narrow streets of a sham village made up of wooden fronts—a stage belonging to a film company. The sergeant still saw the enemy, some fifty policemen gladly taking the part, running toward them, screaming and waving sticks. He wanted a cigarette now but a sergeant on a sidecar cannot smoke. He has to sit erect in his white leather coat, goggles and helmet. The sergeant was sitting erect.

The constable saw the two men first but he didn't say anything. He could have spoken to the sergeant in his normal voice—the engine of a BMW is quiet enough—but the constable didn't say anything. He wanted to go home. His wife would be in bed waiting for him and she was young and warm and cuddly.

Two men were unloading large cartons off a truck parked in front of a small house on the Landsburger dike. They were too busy to see the motorcycle combination bearing down on them. The sergeant had also seen the men and his eyes, shielded behind the goggles, suddenly opened wide. The police only see irregularities: a car weaving in traffic, a brand-new Mercedes with a dirty hippie at the wheel, a man running on the sidewalk, or two men unloading a truck early in the morning. His gloved hand reached out and touched the body of the constable. His other hand pointed at the truck and moved up and down. The constable obeyed.

When the front wheel of the motorcycle almost touched the rear of the truck, the two men shifting cartons inside saw the policemen's helmets. They jumped down, each on one side of the motorcycle combination. The constable tried to grab the man on his side but his gloved hand had no power and the man slipped away. A second later he was clambering down the dike.

The sergeant was tearing off his gloves. The other man was running down the grassy slope of the dike. The policemen were shouting at the fugitives and opening their leather coats to get at their pistols. It took them a while to get the pistols out and by that time the first shot had been fired by the man farthest away. The bullet whined and hit the truck. The constable was firing too now, flat on his stomach and peering over the edge of the dike. He was aiming carefully and his bullet grazed the first fugitive's shoulder.

"Crazy," the sergeant thought. "Crazy! To fire a gun at six o'clock in the morning." He crawled back to the motorcycle, pressed a button and spoke into the large microphone attached to the cycle's tank.

"Headquarters," a quiet voice answered. "Come in, sergeant."

"Request for assistance," the sergeant said. "Landsburger dike. We're engaged in a fire fight."

"I'll see what I can do for you," the voice said, unable to hide its surprise, "but there aren't too many cars about. How many men do you want?"

"Send the lot," the sergeant said. He walked two steps, dropped down to the ground and joined the constable.

"There's another man down there now," the constable said, "and he's firing as well. What *is* this?"

"Do you have any cartridges left?" the sergeant asked.

"One."

"No spare clips?"

"One spare clip, and you?"

"Two shots left and one spare clip. They probably have cases full of ammo down there."

One of the men at the foot of the dike moved and the sergeant fired. The man began to yell.

"I didn't hit him in the stomach, did I?" the sergeant asked the constable. "I was aiming low. I couldn't have hit him in the stomach; it must be his foot or his knee."

The constable raised his head and shouted at the men to surrender but another shot was fired and he had to duck.

The wounded man was still yelling and the others had dropped out of sight. They could hear two sirens coming closer.

"Two cars," the sergeant said; "that's a lot of cars at this time of the day. We're lucky."

The VWs screamed to a stop near the truck and four constables came running toward them.

"Down, down," the sergeant shouted and the men dropped.

"What have you got, sergeant?" a young constable asked, skidding along on his stomach in proper commando style. "Do they have guns down there?"

"Keep your head down; there are two men with pistols and there must be a third pistol near the wounded man. Go back to your car and ask for an ambulance. Ask for the platoon as well."

"All of them?" the constable asked. "There must be forty men in reserve in the barracks."

"No, only a dozen at the most; the others were out on exercise with us all night. Ask for a dozen only and tell them not to send anyone who was on duty last night."

"OK," the constable said and grinned as he ran back to the car. The platoon consisted of cadets only and there was normally little for them to do. He could imagine the excitement in the barracks as the alarm sounded. He remembered his own three months on platoon duty—three months between the end of police school and graduation to constable. Within two minutes they would be tearing about, struggling into their uniforms, grabbing pistols and carbines, and racing out to the armored truck, which, siren howling and lights blazing, would rush them out to the dike.

"Ambulance," he said to the radio, "and the platoon. Sergeant says a dozen men only and not to send anybody who was out tonight. Bring carbines; we're having a proper haw-haw out here."

"Who is wounded?" Headquarters asked. "Police?"

"No."

"OK," Headquarters replied. "Keep us informed. Out."

It took the platoon truck thirteen minutes exactly to arrive. By that time a new volley of shots had been fired and a constable was holding his foot. He was very white in the face and was clenching his teeth; his friend was holding him by the shoulder and talking to him in a soothing voice.

The cadets, commanded by two sergeants, were swarming down the dike from two sides. Four cadets were firing carbines at a wooden shed where the two men were last seen. As the ambulance took the wounded policeman away and another ambulance parked at the curb to wait for the wounded man below, a short rattle increased the tension.

"Tommy gun," the sergeant of the motorcycle said to his mate, "a fucking tommy gun. Did you hear that?"

The constable pointed at the river. "Came from the cruiser over there."

"We'll get everything we have," the sergeant said and sprinted back to his motorcycle radio.

"Tommy gun," he shouted at the radio. "Send everything you can find. We have a wounded constable already and there'll be buckets of blood if this goes on. I don't know how well these cadets have been trained, but bring in the State Water Police and an airplane. They have a boat out there as well, a fast cruiser, and I don't want it to disappear."

"Right," Headquarters said. The buzzers at Headquarters were pressed and every available man, uniform and plainclothes, answered the Grand Alarm. The trucks on the courtyard came to life and the men of the radio room began to telephone all available off-duty personnel. The horsemen were the first to report; they were told to forget about their horses, the distance being too great, and to get into the trucks; an adjutant broke carbines out of a rack and handed them out to whoever presented himself; men helped themselves to spare clips without bothering to sign forms; and the low craft of the State Water Police growled in the harbor as a Piper Cub started its engine at Schiphol airport. Within an hour there were forty policemen on the dike, ten on the river and one in the air. More kept joining them and a commissaris worked out later that some ninety men had taken part in the campaign.

But Grijpstra and de Gier went on sleeping and the commissaris made more coffee and spent time with his turtle. Their names weren't on the lists kept in the radio room and they could only be called if an emergency connected with the death of Tom Wernekink came up. They heard about everything when they arrived at their offices at nine sharp that morning. By that time the fugitives were in custody. Five arrests had been made and an Uzi automatic weapon and five pistols had been confiscated. Detectives were now combing the area, making a house-to-house search, and a dozen fresh policemen were patroling the dike.

Grijpstra went to the radio room to watch the reports coming in on the Teletype. The commissaris was already there.

"Sir," Grijpstra said.

"Morning, adjutant," the commissaris said pleasantly. "Where is your assistant?"

"Reading the reports that have already been distributed," Grijpstra said. "Some show out there! The cartons contained TV sets and other electric stuff. We must have run into something big."

"Yes. The cruiser was full of stolen goods as well. And so were the basements of several houses. The detectives have made some more arrests."

"The Cat," a voice said behind him. "Let's go get the Cat. Now!"

"Quiet," the commissaris said. He had jumped at the sudden shouting close to his ear. "Quiet, de Gier! I am not deaf."

"The Cat," de Gier said. "Let's go!"

De Gier was in the corridor when Grijpstra ran after him. They reached the VW at the same time and de Gier honked the horn impatiently as the constable at the gate came ambling out of his lodge.

"Easy," the constable said. "The alarm is over."

"Not yet," de Gier said and raced the car out the gates.

"I'm getting old," Grijpstra said as de Gier went through the fourth red light. "I saw the reports and my mind didn't click."

"Nonsense. It would have clicked. Buyer and seller of odd lots, bullshit. The bastard was lying through his teeth during that performance in the commissaris' office yesterday. You couldn't know, for you weren't there. The Cat with Boots On, ha, ha!"

"What?" Grijpstra asked.

"He came to see us yesterday. We asked him what he did for a living. Told us a beautiful story about how clever he was. Buys anything going and sells it from a warehouse in town. Odd lot man, bullshit! Sells stolen goods; that's what he does. He must be connected with the men who were arrested this morning. That dike is all connected. They're all in it. That informer too, the Mouse. He must have been right in the middle of it for years, but he never told us anything."

"Tell me more," Grijpstra said. "What was he like? Where did you find him? Did you go to his house?"

De Gier told him as well as he could but he was having some trouble. They had taken a marked car and had the siren and blue light going, but Amsterdam is a busy town at nine-fifteen in the morning and they weren't making much headway. De Gier tried everything he could think of, using the part of the road reserved for the streetcar, the sidewalks and even the footpath of a park, but he kept getting stuck in the tangled traffic. He managed, however, and Grijpstra even heard about Ursula and laughed.

"It would happen to you, wouldn't it?"

"It could have happened to you as well," de Gier shouted. "That woman isn't after any particular kind of man; she just wants a man, a boom-boom man, and you're more boom-boom than I."

Grijpstra slapped his thigh. "Never!"

"Here," de Gier said and braked.

They jumped out of the car and pounded on the door. There was no answer.

"Round the back," Grijpstra shouted.

De Gier ran. The pistol was in his hand. The Cat hadn't reached the river when de Gier shouted at him. The Cat looked very silly with half his mustache shaved off. He was only wearing a pair of jeans and was barefoot.

"Stop," de Gier shouted and fired, pointing the pistol at a cloud.

The Cat stopped.

The Cat surrendered in style to de Gier and four uniformed constables who had come running when they saw the commotion.

"Shit," the Cat said; "you were quick, weren't you, sergeant. Why are you shooting guns in my garden? Tell me the charge."

"Why were you shaving off your mustache?" Grijpstra asked, pulling the Cat's arms round his back and clicking handcuffs on his wrists.

"Got tired of all the hair," the Cat said. "What's the charge? And who are you?"

"Adjutant Grijpstra," Grijpstra said, "at your service. The charge is receiving stolen goods and theft, perhaps, and other crimes maybe. We'll work it out at the station. You'd better get dressed."

"I can't dress with irons on my wrists," the Cat said indignantly.

"We'll take them off again."

De Gier pointed his pistol at the Cat as Grijpstra took off the handcuffs in the Cat's bedroom. The Cat opened cupboards and drawers and dressed leisurely.

"Don't you want your golden suit and your boots?" de Gier asked.

"No. But I want to shave off the rest of my mustache."

"No," Grijpstra said, "not yet. I'd like the commissaris to see you like this, and the photographer. Fighting on the dike, arresting thieves, a tommy gun blazing away with the street full of police and detectives going from house to house, and here you are shaving off your mustache. And you run—in your jeans and bare feet—when we come to see you. I think it's strange, don't you?"

"No," the Cat said, "and I want some coffee before I go. Ursula!"

Ursula, dressed in a housecoat, came from the kitchen. Her long legs were partly uncovered and the full breasts were standing under the flimsy garment.

"Watch it," Grijpstra said as de Gier's eyes strayed.

"Yes, watch it, sergeant," the Cat said; "you have a murderous weapon in your hand and your finger is very close to the trigger, and the barrel is very close to my chest. Besides, she is mine, not yours."

"Mine," Ursula said, "what mine? I'm not a cow. And what's all this, Cat? Are they taking you away?"

"I am afraid we are, miss," Grijpstra said.

"Who are you?"

"Detective-Adjutant Grijpstra, Amsterdam municipal police."

Ursula inclined her head and the long hair fell over her face. She shook it back.

"Look after him, adjutant," she said. "He is nice and he means well. What are they charging you with, Cat?"

"It's my mind," the Cat said; "they don't like what's going on in my mind. I'm different, and they represent the common law. I am not common; that's my trouble."

"Were you in the fight this morning?" Grijpstra asked.

The Cat laughed. "Me? I have never been in a fight in my life. I buy goods and I sell goods and I talk and listen a lot."

"But you are friendly with the people on the dike," de Gier said, "and they *did* fight. They even wounded two policemen, I hear, one in the foot and one in the arm. They were firing away as if there were a war on. And the dike is full of stolen goods. I would like to go through your house."

"No," the Cat said. "Your rank is too low. You can't search the house without a warrant. You're lucky I let you in as it is. Get a warrant, sergeant."

"Don't be silly," Ursula said. "There's nothing in the house."

"OK," the Cat said and smiled. "Search the place if you like."

De Gier found nothing. "Where is your warehouse?"

"In town, but it's no use going there; it's locked and I have the key. I'll go with you if you like."

"Later," Grijpstra said.

"I want my coffee."

"Later. We have coffee at the station. Sorry, miss, for the intrusion. We'll have to go now."

"Be nice to him," Ursula said.

8

BICKERS ISLAND USED TO BE A FORGOTTEN CORNER OF THE city of Amsterdam. Its maze of narrow streets, quays lined with high sixteenth-century warehouses, wharves where hundreds of years ago the flat-bottomed sailing and cargo vessels were built, canals, gardens, and even a few merchant mansions, had all rotted, sagged and fallen together into crumbling heaps where rats were no longer frightened of the few people who refused to move. But the city had come to life again and cared about itself. The island had been rediscovered by architects and artists, backed by the Public Works Department, and gradually the warehouses were being restored, the gardens cleaned up and replanted with shrubs and trees and the canals dredged. It was still a quiet place, however, for it was out of the way; one could walk about in peace and concentration without jumping about like a demented monkey for fear of being crushed by the onslaught of modern traffic.

The commissaris, having stumbled onto the island during a murderous adventure when he was still a sub-inspector in his early twenties, had made the place his favorite haunt. He could often be found there, during weekends and holidays, wandering about the alleys, sitting on a wooden bench in a public garden, standing on the quay craning his neck to admire a gable top or dreaming in the courtyard of a deserted mansion. He always ended up in the same small pub, the last of its kind, where a very old landlord—a living skeleton—still poured jenever for his few guests from a stone bottle. It made a gay tinkling sound as he filled the delicate tulip-shaped glasses with the amber-colored, syrupy, almost frozen, explosive. The tinkling sound was caused by a narrow metal spout, screwed onto the bottle and as old as the pub itself. The pub was three times as old as its present owner and its weird lugubrious atmosphere never failed to excite the commissaris, whose pleasures, although few, were always intense.

It was five o'clock in the afternoon, on the day after the arrest of the Cat and the release of Mary van Krompen, set free by the commissaris himself. He had carried her bag to the door himself and sent her home in his own chauffeur-driven car. The day had been spent so far in clearing up odds and ends, left over by the commotion on the dike. Apart from the Cat's, nine arrests had now been made, and most of the detectives on the Force were engaged in typing reports after having interrogated their suspects. A disturbed mayor had called a meeting at City Hall where he asked the chief constable questions and later the commissaris and two of his colleagues were summoned by telephone to come and explain how such a boisterous act of aggression could have occurred in their pleasant and tolerant town. The commissaris hadn't said much apart from a remark that he meant to go into the matter further.

The four guests had the small pub to themselves. At the request of the commissaris the landlord had locked his door and hung out a dirty crumpled cardboard sign saying that the pub was closed because of death. The owner had written the sign thirty years ago when his wife died.

De Gier, impeccable in a new blue denim suit, made by a Turkish tailor—an illegal immigrant and a friend—sat on a high barstool, studying a little man with a pencil-lined mustache and a bald head sitting opposite and below him on a low chair. Grijpstra was leaning against the bar, holding a small glass of jenever in his hand and chewing a sausage. He was also studying the man on the low chair. The commissaris was looking out the window, contemplating the shape of the wreck of a botter and imagining what it would have been like to go to sea to catch a load of shrimp in such a small craft, thirty feet long at the most, with only two men in the crew and no engine to help maneuver the vessel.

The botter, its mast still intact, had been moored at the quay for as long as he could remember and he had often thought that he should find out who owned her. He could buy the boat, have her repaired—rebuilt if necessary—and take her sailing on the great inland lake with de Gier and Grijpstra as a crew.

He smiled at himself. A dream of course. The pain in his legs, his everlasting rheumatic affliction would kill the fun. It would be worse on the water.

The pub was very quiet. The small man got up and, looking at the landlord, placed his glass on the counter. The landlord grabbed the bottle and the jenever tinkled into the glass. The small man sat down again. Nobody said anything.

"Stop staring," the little man suddenly squeaked. "Stare at something else, will you? Look out the window. Look at the nice botter the commissaris is admiring. Isn't it a nice botter?"

Grijpstra and de Gier stared.

"Isn't it?" the small man said hopefully.

"Mouse," Grijpstra said, his deep voice filling the small room, "tell us why you didn't tell us."

The Mouse looked at Grijpstra and wondered if he should ask, "What?" He didn't, but got up instead, intending to place his glass on the counter again.

Grijpstra stopped him.

"Can't I drink?"

"No," Grijpstra said. "Tell us why you didn't tell us. You can drink later. At home or somewhere. Here you have had enough."

The Mouse licked his lips. "I'm thirsty; my mouth is all leathery. Can I have a lemonade or something?"

Grijpstra looked at the landlord and nodded.

The Mouse sipped his lemonade.

"Well?" de Gier asked.

But the Mouse said nothing.

The commissaris stopped looking at the botter and joined his two colleagues at the bar, climbing painfully onto a stool and rubbing his legs when he had managed the feat.

"Well, Mouse?" the commissaris asked.

The Mouse put his glass back and waved his hands.

"You have nothing on me, sir," he squeaked indignantly. "All right, so I'm an informer. But I am not *obliged* to inform, am I?"

"You are obliged," Grijpstra boomed, "to inform the

police if you have knowledge of a crime. You live on the dike and you were right bang in the middle of all the stealing and receiving and the whatever-else-goes-on there. You saw it all; you helped them most probably. And you didn't tell."

"Can you *prove* I was in it?" the Mouse asked fearfully and enthusiastically at the same time. "Did you find anything in my house? Did you meet anyone who said anything about me that can incriminate me? Did you? Did you?"

Grijpstra was silent and de Gier adjusted the colored scarf that he had knotted around his neck.

"You didn't," the Mouse said triumphantly. "You did NOT."

De Gier put his glass down and the jenever bottle tinkled. Grijpstra lit a cigar, a fat black cigar, and a cloud of vile smoke drifted in the direction of the commissaris, who began to cough.

"Sorry, sir," Grijpstra said and patted his superior on the back; "I'll put it out."

"No, no," the commissaris said as he stopped coughing and looked at the Mouse. "Mouse," he said, "we pay you. And if you take money you are under obligation. You have to tell. You should have refused the money but you took it. Taxpayers' money."

"Ha," the Mouse said.

The commissaris shook his head. "No, Mouse. It may seem silly to you but taxpayers' money is holy money. To me it is. And to many others. More others than you expect. This is a decent city. If something is given, something is expected. You failed. But you can still make up for it."

"What if I don't," the Mouse said defiantly.

"I don't think much will happen if you don't," the commissaris said softly, "not just now. Later maybe."

"You are threatening me."

"No, Mouse. I am not threatening. There is the Law."

"Ha," the Mouse said but his voice sounded sad.

"Not, 'Ha,'" the commissaris said. "And I don't mean the law of our law books. The law books only show the shadow of the law, the law as we can understand it, but our understanding changes all the time so the law books change as well. I mean the Law."

"God?" the Mouse asked; "you talking about God?"

"No, Mouse. I don't know God."

"I think you are talking about God," the Mouse said stubbornly.

"Not having met God, I can't talk about Him," the commissaris said, "but I have seen a little of the Law. The Law is very beautiful."

The Mouse put his glass on the counter, waited, and drank the lemonade in one gulp. He sat down again and began to rub his bald head.

"The Law," he said hesitantly.

De Gier wanted to say something but the commissaris raised his hand. Grijpstra inhaled his cigar. He began to cough and threw the cigar on the floor and stamped it out.

"Right," the Mouse said, "I'll tell. But I won't repeat it in court. It isn't a statement. You can't hold me to it. Right?"

"Yes," the commissaris said.

"And I don't want money. No obligation. Right?"

"Yes."

"OK," the Mouse said and the pub changed. It seemed much lighter now and de Gier was scratching his back and grinning. Grijpstra lit a fresh cigar and the commissaris smiled. Even the skeleton behind the counter relaxed and the jenever bottle's tinkle had its old happy gurgly ring.

"It's the Cat," the Mouse said. "The Cat is a genius. I like him. I admire him too. He is the blessing of the dike.

But it couldn't have been as bad as on the dike. It made me sick; it made everybody sick."

"And then the Cat came," the commissaris said.

"Yes, sir. The Cat got a rotten little house and fixed it up. We looked on and nobody helped him at first, but he asked advice, you see. He would come up to you and ask you how he should do this and how he should do that. Before we knew it we were all helping him."

"Good," the commissaris said.

"Yes. And we got to know him and he got to know us. And his girl, Ursula, would make tea in the garden. We would sit there and drink it and then go back to work. We had that house fixed up in a few weeks: new beams, a new roof—a new wall even—proper brick laying and plastering. And we painted all the woodwork and tiled the floor. All the time the Cat was asking us about what we were doing on the dike."

"You weren't only drinking and boasting," de Gier said; "you were stealing and burglarizing as well."

"Sure, sure," the Mouse said. "Not me, mind you. I have my pension and I'm quiet. The others were."

"Sure," Grijpstra said.

"So we told him and he listened very carefully and didn't say much. For months he didn't say much. Even when we began to fix up our own houses and he was helping *us*."

"Where did you get your materials," the commissaris asked.

"Stole it, sir. Some of it came from the river but all the good stuff we stole and that's how it all started. He told us to organize ourselves. We wanted a lot of paint, for instance. In the old days we would have stolen a can here and a can there, but he told us not to be silly. If you steal one miserable can of paint and you're caught, it's proper theft all right and they throw the book at you. He told us to steal everything we wanted in one go and we made a plan, or rather, he made a plan. We began to watch a wholesale place in town, checking the times of their delivery trucks. Then we lifted a whole truck. We knew what the truck was carrying before we lifted it. It was a beautiful bit of work. Someone got the keys copied while the driver was in a café, weeks before we did the actual job. All we had to do that particular day was to wait for the driver to make a small delivery, jump into the truck and drive off. Nice and quiet. No rush. No going through red lights. We had another truck waiting and we changed the load, leaving the stolen truck neatly parked at the curb somewhere, and drove home in the other truck. A hired truck. The job took a little time and a little money but it gave us a wallop of a profit. We couldn't use all that paint so the Cat sold what was left. And he got a good price. And he shared it."

"How much did he take for himself?" Grijpstra asked.

"A quarter."

"He was being straight with you, wasn't he?"

"Certainly," the Mouse said indignantly.

"Did he take part in the actual theft?"

"No. He told us from the beginning that he would never do any stealing. He only sold the stuff, and only if the job had been properly planned by himself."

"Go on."

"Well, that gave us some self-respect, just what we needed. And we went on from there. We got a few truckloads of lumber and some roof tiles. We even got tools, lovely tools. The only thing we paid for was cement, since we didn't want to steal a cement truck; they're too obvious with their turning tanks."

"And nobody talked?" de Gier asked.

"No. Never. I didn't talk either. The Cat was giving me a bad conscience."

"Did he know you are an informer?" Grijpstra asked.

"No. Nobody knows. My wife doesn't know. I don't even know myself. I don't want to know. And I won't inform again."

"You turned that old friend of yours in," Grijpstra said; "that wasn't so long ago. And you told us about the escaped burglar."

"I know, I know," the Mouse squeaked. "I had to do something every once in a while, but it's all over now. Never again. And they had nothing to do with us or the Cat. You would have caught them anyway."

"The Cat is caught," the commissaris said.

"Yes. Something went wrong. He warned them, you know."

"What went wrong?"

"The boasting. It never stopped. The Cat couldn't kill it. We got our self-respect back and we were doing real proper jobs but it wasn't enough. Not all of us, mind you; some of us knew how to handle the new situation. But some couldn't. They wanted to be real gangsters and were going to town all the time to watch the pictures. All these old French gangster movies. The silent types with the guns. Pistols and tommy guns, fast cars and nice women with short skirts and a lot of tit on them. They thought they had to be like that. All silly imagination and film nonsense. There are no such people. The Cat told them and I told them too, but they wouldn't believe it. They were stealing truckloads, big truckloads by then. Containers. Expensive stuff. Color TVs and electrical household goods. Freezers and big stereo radio combinations and stoves and washing machines. The lot. The Cat was selling it for real money, and handing it out as fast as he got it. They would all meet in somebody's house—like a party—and he would say, 'You did this so I think you get so much,' 'you did that so I think you get so much.' He would look around and if everybody said OK he handed over the money."

"Anybody ever put up a stink?" Grijpstra asked.

"No. The Cat's propositions were good. They wanted him to ask them for their opinions. That's all they wanted, and he did."

"What did *you* do?" the commissaris asked.

"I studied the truck drivers, followed them about, found out where they stopped on the way. I also got their keys and had them copied. One of the men used to be a locksmith. We would go in my car and follow the truck; I would lift the keys, rush them back to the car, and he would copy them. I would put them back again. But I never did the heavy work."

"Ever get into trouble?"

"No, sir," the Mouse said proudly. "I have an ordinary car and I look ordinary. Nobody notices me much."

"Have a drink."

"Thank you, sir."

The four glasses were lined up and the landlord filled them. They raised their glasses and drank.

"So tell us about what went wrong."

"Yes, sir. The boasting as I said. Acting big. Some of them began to swagger about. The houses were all refurnished with wall-to-wall carpets, color TVs, new curtains and furniture and so on. And the gardens were fixed up. And then they bought clothes. And cars, nice cars. Then they began to buy guns. Somebody went to Belgium and came back with an automatic pistol. He showed it around and then some others wanted arms as well. We had been working on an old cruiser, putting in a new engine, and they thought they might do some thieving off ships; that's why they got the tommy gun. Frightened of the tough sailors, I suppose. The Cat was dead against it. His plans never called for firearms. No violence. Not even when I couldn't get the keys off one particular truck driver. The Cat used a girl that time. I found out that the driver liked to pick up girls on the way, so the Cat found a nice prostitute in town, made up to her and offered her a good share. She got herself in the way of the driver and he took her; then she suggested parking the truck in a convenient place and going into the bushes. While they were busy out there we emptied the truck."

"We?" the commissaris asked.

"No, not me. I was driving behind the truck in my own car but I only hung about, in case something went wrong. But nothing went wrong. He came back with the girl and didn't even know he'd lost his cargo; I picked up the girl at the next stop, while he was in the toilet. Ha, he must have pulled a funny face when he realized the girl was gone and his lovely load of washing machines as well. Forty washing machines. The Cat had his full crew working that time."

"And the Cat wasn't there?"

"No, sir. Never. He thought it out at home, working with the information we brought in. We didn't mind. He was giving us something to do and paying well. We didn't want him to stick his neck out."

"And he didn't approve of the firearms, did he?"

"No. But I don't think he was too worried. His plans never called for firearms and there were enough older and stable people to keep the others in check. It was only when your silly motorcops blundered into us that it all went wrong."

"You people wounded two constables," the commissaris said.

"Yes," the Mouse said, "how are they? The constables?"

"One is all right; his shoulder is hurt but it isn't serious—he'll be on duty again in a few weeks—but the other is bad. Some of the bones in his foot are smashed. He'll limp for the rest of his life and he'll have to leave the Force."

"Shame," the Mouse said and looked as if he meant it.

"But why did they start shooting?" de Gier asked. "Bloody silly, wasn't it? Theft is a crime, of course, but you people never threatened anyone or hurt anyone or committed any serious offense. If they had surrendered to those motorcops they would only have been charged with theft. Why use firearms? Bloody idiotic! The public prosecutor will make mincemeat of them; they'll be in jail for years and years now."

"Yes, I know," the Mouse said sadly; "they wouldn't listen. Boasting. I told you before. They were saying that they would never surrender to the fuzz. The young ones—you see—were talking about getting away and taking the money to some foreign country and living the life. All nonsense. It's the movies; they shouldn't show movies like that. Some people can't take it."

"Tommy gun, indeed," Grijpstra said.

The Mouse suddenly smiled.

"Why do you smile, Mouse?"

"I was thinking about that gun, sir," the Mouse said. "Very dramatic, that was. I remember the man who brought it from Belgium coming in with it. He was wearing a suit and a hat, just like those French gangsters do, and he had the tommy gun in two parts. He stood in the middle of the room and stuck the clip into the gun. It clicked, a heavy sort of click. And suddenly everybody shut up and looked at him. Very impressive, you know. Even I was impressed."

"I am glad he never hit anyone with that tool," the commissaris said.

"He only fired once, sir, and he aimed high. He just wanted to make a noise."

"Did he tell you?"

"I heard," the Mouse said modestly. "I heard."

"How much money went through the Cat's hands?" Grijpstra asked.

The Mouse looked careful. "I worked it out once, about two million, I think. But he had other things going as well. He was talking of retiring next year and wanted us to retire as well. He wanted to go abroad."

"Hey," de Gier said, "that girl you were telling us about— the one who seduced the truck driver and kept him in the bushes for a while—that wasn't Ursula, was it?"

"No, no," the Mouse said, "not Ursula. A prostitute from town, didn't I tell you?"

"Yes," de Gier said, "but you might have been mixed up a little."

"No. I wasn't mixed up. I only get mixed up when you all sit and stare at me as if I'm some silly animal in the zoo or a fish in an aquarium. Ursula wouldn't do, you see; she is too tall. The truck driver would see her in town and remember."

De Gier looked relieved and the Mouse saw it and grinned.

"You like her, do you? Careful, sergeant." The Mouse wagged a finger.

"Careful of what?"

"She is very big. She'll open up and whoosh, there'll be nothing left of you."

Grijpstra and the commissaris laughed and the Mouse,

happy with his success, jumped up and doubled over with mirth.

"OK, OK, OK," de Gier said.

"Never mind, sergeant," the Mouse said; "I was only joking. She is a nice girl. You should try, you know, maybe you'll be lucky. She isn't faithful and the Cat doesn't mind."

"He'll be away for a while," Grijpstra said thoughtfully and looked at de Gier.

The commissaris waved a small hand.

"All right, we know about the sergeant's weaknesses. Thank you, Mouse; we know a little more now. You didn't tell us what your information is worth to you."

"No, sir," the Mouse said nervously, "no money. I am through. If ever you want some friendly advice let me know, but, if I give it, it'll be free. For nothing. And I'll only give it to you, or to the adjutant or the sergeant. No one else."

"What are you going to do now, Mouse?" Grijpstra asked.

"Fish," the Mouse said. "You fish too, I know. I have found some good spots; we can go together sometime. Not on the dike. I don't want to be seen with the police."

"What else?"

"Nothing," the Mouse said. "I'm getting old. I'll be seventy in two years' time."

The Mouse looked happy now and his small beady eyes were glinting. He called for a round and put a note on the counter. "You too," he said to the skeleton and the skeleton poured an extra glass and raised it solemnly.

"You feel better now, Mouse?" Grijpstra asked, his voice sounding almost tender. That's the way he talks to his small son, de Gier thought. Grijpstra was fond of his small son who often came to Headquarters as he and de Gier were about to leave their office for the day. He'd pull Grijpstra's jacket and force him to leave his papers alone and go home.

"There's one little last question, Mouse," the commissaris said.

"I know," the Mouse said. "I was wondering about it. Thought you would have mentioned it at the beginning, when you had me in a corner."

"Wernekink," the commissaris said.

The Mouse was shaking his head. "Don't know, sir. Told you before, didn't I. Nobody on the dike knew him well, except the Cat, and the Cat doesn't kill."

"You're sure?"

"Absolutely. The Cat was upset about Wernekink's death. Really upset. I went to see him, since I was curious too. I thought some of the fast lads might be suspects—the lads with the suits and the hats and the firearms—but they couldn't have done it. I know them all and they don't shoot well. No practice. None of them had even been in the army. Army didn't want them. Misfits, all of them. They can pull a trigger but they can't hit anyone between the eyes."

"They got the constables all right," Grijpstra said.

"Pure luck. They were emptying one clip after another and that way you'll always hit something; the dike was blue with uniforms."

"Yes," the commissaris said, "the ballistics man was telling me the constables were hit by bullets that had hit something else first."

"You see," the Mouse said.

"What's your theory about Wernekink's death?" de Gier asked.

The Mouse was shaking his head again. "Don't know. No idea. I have thought about it and thought about it but there was no reason. No motive. Who would kill a man who knew nobody and who wanted nothing. He didn't even want the girl next door and she was pretty enough."

"You don't think that lesbian lady did it?"

"No, no," the Mouse said. "Mary is all right. She's a nice pleasant soul who cares for people. And she is happy with that other woman; they are always together, shopping together, going for drives together. They even go rowing together on the river." The Mouse shuddered.

"You got the shakes?" Grijpstra asked. "You aren't drinking too much, are you?"

"No. It's these lesbians. They upset me. I can't understand it. Unnatural, isn't it?"

De Gier laughed at the Mouse's discomfort. "I think five percent of all people on earth have homosexual tendencies," he said. "That's five in a hundred, a lot of people. Too many to be unnatural."

"I don't like it," the Mouse said.

"Why?"

"Makes me feel silly. I am a man, and women need men. But these women don't need men."

"You are close to seventy," the commissaris said. "Aren't you getting a little too old for that sort of thing now, Mouse?"

"Yes, sir," the Mouse said, "but it's the idea."

The commissaris clambered down from his stool and they had a last drink, standing in a little group near the counter. The Mouse put his glass down and pointed at the botter lying outside in the canal. He told an interesting story about the vessel and asked them to look at the ornament on the rudder, a reclining lion, stretched out with its head on its paws. Bits of gold paint were still visible on the sculpture. De Gier said something about the lion and the commissaris and Grijpstra were listening to him. When they looked around the Mouse was gone. They hadn't heard the door. The old landlord hadn't seen him leave either.

"That's the way he always goes," Grijpstra said, "sneaky little fellow."

"Not a bad chap," de Gier said.

"No," the commissaris said, "but he should have warned us about the firearms. He could have done it in some delicate way and we could have organized a small raid and confiscated the pistols and the tommy gun. That constable may lose the use of his foot. I wish I'd known about the firearms."

"You don't mind about the paint and the TVs and the washing machines, do you, sir?" Grijpstra asked. "I mean, you don't mind very much."

The commissaris grunted.

⦀⦀⦀ 9 ⫽⫽⫽

THE COMMISSARIS GRUNTED. HIS HEAD THROBBED AND HE was thirsty. His legs hurt but the pain in his head was worse, much worse. There were ants in his head, digging narrow tunnels through his brain. He could feel them scratching the inside of his skull and turning round to dig fresh tunnels. He had already emptied a liter bottle of orange juice but the dry grating feeling in his mouth hadn't changed. He hadn't spoken yet that morning and he wasn't quite sure whether he could.

Grijpstra and de Gier were seated. They had stood around at first but when the commissaris had waved and nodded, they had each taken a chair. They had said good morning and were waiting. It was the commissaris' turn to speak but he still had a few seconds' grace. He used the few seconds to criticize himself. He shouldn't have allowed himself to get drunk. But he had. It had been a bad day, of course—a day of pain—but he should be used to pain by now.

He had gone home after the meeting with the Mouse, arriving by eight o'clock, still in time for a late dinner and the company of his wife's two sisters. There had been wine on the table and the commissaris had served himself the best part of two bottles. The ladies had talked so much that his drunkenness wasn't noticed. And brandy with the coffee, a quarter bottle? Or half a bottle perhaps? He had reached his bed by himself but his wife must have undressed him. He couldn't remember. But he did remember that he hadn't undressed himself.

It didn't happen very often, once or twice a year. But it shouldn't happen at all, the commissaris thought. But there was the pain, of course. The eternal pain in his legs. Alcohol stops the pain; it never fails. Perhaps he could excuse himself.

"De Gier," the commissaris croaked.

"Sir," de Gier said pleasantly.

"Some orange juice," the commissaris croaked. "In the fridge over there. Pour it for me, please, and get me some coffee too!"

De Gier poured the orange juice and Grijpstra left the room. He returned with a tray and three paper cups.

The commissaris felt a little better. "Now," he said, "one of the inspectors on duty last night phoned me this morning. It seems you made two arrests. I thought you had gone home. Tell me about it."

He was looking at Grijpstra and Grijpstra sat up. "Nothing to do with the death on the dike, sir."

"No?" the commissaris asked. "But that's the case we are working on."

"I know, sir, but we didn't go home. We came back here."

"Played drums?" the commissaris asked and managed to smile. He had finished the orange juice and looked helplessly at de Gier, who got up and refilled the glass.

"Yes, sir," Grijpstra said. "De Gier played his flute and I banged about for a while. We also read the reports of the day."

"Yes, yes. So what happened."

"Remember the old lady who was found in the canal, sir?"

"Yes, I read about it, but I didn't see the corpse."

"I saw the corpse," de Gier said.

The commissaris shook his head.

"I know, sir," de Gier said. "I don't like corpses but when I read through the report the name of the dead woman seemed familiar and I finally remembered that I knew her."

The commissaris looked interested.

"She made a complaint about the man she lived with," de Gier said. "About six months ago. I dealt with the case. She said he had been threatening her."

"Had he?"

"Yes, sir. He had beaten her up too. She had a black eye. But there was no case. When I saw her at her home she said she had made a mistake."

"And the black eye?"

"The doorpost," Grijpstra said. "They always walk into the doorpost. Amsterdam is full of doorposts."

"Yes," de Gier said, "the doorpost. I talked to her and tried to reason with her but she was a funny old lady. She was a little drunk that time."

"So there was no case," the commissaris said and noticed

with some pleasure that the words came out fairly easily now. "No complaint, no case."

"But then she died," de Gier said, "and I saw the corpse. There was a wound on the head. The Water Police thought the wound might have been caused by a screw on one of their own patrol boats or by a river barge. She was found near the Brouwersgracht/Prinsengracht bridge. There's a lot of traffic there."

"The tourists' boats," the commissaris said.

"Yes. I thought they might be right and it wasn't our case anyway, so I didn't do anything. But last night we read through the reports again and saw that the death had been written off as accidental."

"So?"

"We thought we might as well go into it," Grijpstra said. "De Gier said that the lady wasn't the sort who would fall into the canal. And there was the wound."

"But the inspector says you arrested two men and they confessed," the commissaris said and tried to light a cigar. His hand trembled and Grijpstra jumped up and flicked his lighter.

"A very easy case, sir," Grijpstra said. "We went to the house where she used to live and the man wasn't in. He is a painter, a tall man with long gray hair. I am sure you know him yourself. He paints in the street and sells his work to tourists. Clever portraits—a bit wishy-washy but good enough to ask money for—and he also paints houses and bridges."

"Wears a necklace of colored pebbles?"

"That's the man, sir."

"I know him," the commissaris said. "He never used to have a license and has been fined a few times, but he's got a license now. Man with a red nose. He drinks."

"That's right, sir," Grijpstra said.

The commissaris felt a slight wave of pity.

"So we went to the nearest pub and there he was."

"Yes," de Gier said, "with his friend, a young fellow."

"What pub?" the commissaris asked.

"The Emperor, sir."

The commissaris grimaced. He knew the Emperor, a long narrow room furnished with the latest in bad taste. A frilly pub with cretonne lampshades, pink lights, imitation crystal ornaments, full-size mirrors and tables with plastic tops that looked a little like marble. The commissaris also knew the Emperor's reputation.

"You know the place, don't you, sir?" Grijpstra asked.

"Yes. Where the gay boys pick up the shopkeepers from the provinces."

"But the gay boys aren't gay at all," de Gier said. "They are hoodlums who squeeze the country boys dry and blackmail them if they can."

"Didn't the owner lose his license?" the commissaris asked.

"Yes, sir. But the new owner is just as bad."

"Perhaps the chief constable should have the place closed," the commissaris said. "I'll mention it some time."

"They'll go somewhere else, sir."

"True," the commissaris said. "Go on. A young fellow you said."

The two detectives looked out the window.

"We had a theory, sir," Grijpstra said after a while.

"Quite. The old man liked the young fellow and they murdered the old lady together. Where did the young fellow stay?"

"With the painter, sir. Has been living there for over a year."

"And the old lady objected so they beat her up and she came to us. Then they talked to her again and she withdrew the charge."

"And they murdered her six months later," de Gier said, "but we had to prove it."

"Did he remember you?" the commissaris said.

"That's what made it difficult, sir," de Gier said. "He remembered my face the minute I sat down next to him."

"Did he think you were after him?"

"No; that's what made it easy again. I bought him a drink and Grijpstra bought him a drink and the young fellow bought us a drink and we laughed a lot."

"You didn't mention the old lady of course," the commissaris said. He was feeling much better now; the ants had gone and he wasn't so thirsty anymore. He rubbed his legs.

"No, sir. We let them talk. They wanted us to mention the old lady, for they knew the Water Police were ready to close the case, or had already done so."

"He bragged," Grijpstra said; "that young fellow bragged. He thought he was awfully clever. The painter makes a lot of money and I am sure he was getting most of it. A sharp dresser, that boy. A four-hundred-guilder leather jacket, hand-embroidered shirt, heavy golden bracelets, six-hundred-guilder watch, rings, suede boots, and a fifty-guilder haircut. He talked a lot, that boy."

"And he trapped himself, did he?"

"Yes, sir," de Gier said. "It was unbelievably easy. He told us where the body was found—the exact spot—Brouwersgracht/Prinsengracht bridge. But the report said that they had only been told that the body was found somewhere in the Prinsengracht. The Prinsengracht is a long canal. It starts at the Amstel River and it ends at the IJ River. We had read the Water Police report of the questioning. It never mentioned the bridge, so he couldn't know."

"You arrested them straightaway?"

"I took the young fellow and Grijpstra got a patrol car for the painter."

"They confessed quickly?"

"The painter confessed in the patrol car, sir," Grijpstra said. "The young fellow took an hour. They killed her together because they couldn't get rid of her in any other way. She had threatened to go to the tax people to disclose the painter's real income. He only declares one tenth of what he gets, of course."

"I don't think the tax people would have been very interested," the commissaris said. "They're after bigger fish."

Grijpstra sighed.

"I think she loved the old fellow," de Gier said. "She was only threatening, hoping he would tell the boy to go."

"How old is the boy?" the commissaris asked.

"Over twenty-one."

"No loose ends in the case, are there?"

"No, sir. The confessions are signed. We found the weapon as well. The Water Police dragged it up this morning. I watched them do it. First they found twelve bicycles, then a perambulator, and then half a ton of tin cans, and bicycles and bottles and furniture. But they found the pipe as well, a solid metal pipe a foot long. The doctor says it matches the wound."

"How did you know where to look?"

"The old man told us; they threw it in with the body. The body should have floated away but it got stuck on something, a bicycle probably."

"Congratulations," the commissaris said. "That's one

death solved. The girl with the heroin is no problem either; the doctor is sure she gave herself an overdose."

"That leaves us with Wernekink," Grijpstra said.

"Brilliant work," the commissaris said, "but we are still left with a killer. A killer with no apparent motive. Go think about it. If you can't find him nobody can. I'll sit here and think as well but I'm getting old and my head hurts. Is there any more orange juice, de Gier?"

They were in the corridor a minute later and de Gier stopped in front of the large mirror that the chief constable had installed so that the men could check their appearance. He stopped and waved at himself. Grijpstra stood next to him and saluted.

A constable stopped and asked them if they were all right.

"No," Grijpstra said, "we are mad. Hehehehehe."

The constable came to attention and farted.

"Don't do that!" de Gier said.

"I am mad too," the constable said. "Hehehehehe."

///// 10 /////

"YES," GRIJPSTRA SAID LOUDLY AND HIT THE LARGEST OF his drums with some force.

De Gier looked pained.

"Don't," he said. "Please."

Grijpstra put his drumstick down. "No?" he asked heavily and pushed a hand through the short gray stubble on his skull.

"No," de Gier said and made a gesture as if he were holding a tall slim girl by the middle and shaking her. "No, Grijpstra."

Grijpstra got up and walked to the center of their large room, which de Gier was dominating with his elegant presence.

"No," de Gier said again. "We are in the right mood now. We pulled that other thing off. You played it down so that you could impress the commissaris but the fact is that we did well. And if we can do one thing we can do another. This Wernekink business is annoying me; it's annoying you too and it *was* annoying the commissaris. He's got something else on his mind now so it's all up to us. And we are in the right mood. If we think properly and use the information we have in the right way we can crack the case. I am sure of it. But we can't do anything if you're going to hit that drum with all the force you have in you."

Grijpstra's mouth was open.

"Close your mouth," de Gier said.

"What's the matter with you?" Grijpstra asked. "What's all this cleverness all of a sudden? We arrested two stupid murderers because they committed a stupid murder and we used ordinary straightforward police routine. What are you puffing yourself up for? And what's this about the commissaris?"

"A hangover," de Gier said. "He must have got himself drunk after we left the Mouse yesterday. His rheumatism must have been worse than usual; he has been very sickly lately. All he wants to do now is sit behind his desk and drink orange juice and coffee and maybe smoke a few cigars. Later today he'll go home and go to bed. He'll be asleep because his wife will give him a pill."

"He'll still be concerned," Grijpstra said. "He'll think and he'll come up with something."

De Gier smiled and put a long hand on Grijpstra's shoulder. "He'll think but we can do something. What are we going to do?"

"You name it," Grijpstra said. "You name it."

"You can play your drum, but softly. You can play this as well, look."

De Gier had gone to the corner of their office and stood in front of the curtain covering a recess where they kept their coats in winter. Grijpstra, his low forehead wrinkled, was staring at him.

"You're irritating me, de Gier."

"I know. Look."

De Gier pulled the curtain aside and Grijpstra uttered a deep throaty sound.

"You know what this is?"

The object, attached to a metal rod resting on a three-pronged, rubber-capped base, looked like a fat cucumber with a number of ridges.

"Nice," Grijpstra said and picked up his drumstick again.

"No, no," de Gier said. "It's got its own stick."

He gave him a heavy short stick and put the instrument close to the set of drums. "Sit down and see if you can do something with it. I have tried but it isn't for me. Perhaps I can use the flute with it. Go ahead."

Grijpstra rustled on the middle drum with his left hand, tried a roll on the smallest drum, hit a cymbal and suddenly hit the cucumber. The sound was electric, changing the atmosphere of the room immediately and completely. De Gier had his flute to his mouth and breathed a tremulous obbligato into the raucous exchange of drums and cucumber. Grijpstra sat up and began a rapid pounding on the big drum; de Gier's obbligato continued but became less complicated and somewhere in the next few bars a shuffle formed itself, which went on for some ten minutes with the cucumber sound as its main pivot. They stopped because someone had come into the room. They began to laugh at the same time.

"I'm glad to see you are happy," young Cardozo said, "but the chief inspector would be grateful if you could be happy quietly for a while."

"Sure," Grijpstra said and got up. "Thanks, de Gier—a most extraordinary sound."

"What does it remind you of?" de Gier asked.

"What, the sound?"

"The sound."

"Of a dream," Grijpstra said after a while, "but a dream I couldn't remember when I woke up. I remembered I had a dream—a very important dream—but every time I tried to remember a detail it slipped away. Slowly, but quick enough to be beyond reach. You know it is there but you can't touch it."

Cardozo was still in the room. De Gier turned toward the young constable-detective and smiled. Cardozo looked sweet, with his long hair and corduroy suit and large deerlike eyes.

"Go on," Cardozo said; "never mind the chief inspector. If you play a little softer he can't hear. I'm sorry I interrupted you. What's that new instrument?"

"Don't know," de Gier said. "I found it secondhand in a music shop. The man said he bought it from a bankrupt pop group."

"Expensive?" Grijpstra asked.

"Fairly."

"Good," Grijpstra said. "It's worth it."

"I paid," de Gier said.

"Of course." Grijpstra glared at Cardozo. "Have you got nothing to do, Cardozo?"

"No, but I would like to do something."

"That's the proper attitude," de Gier said. "Get some coffee then. You are the youngest member of the murder squad, so you can get the coffee, and pay for it too."

"Certainly," Cardozo said. "Right away."

He came back with the coffee and Grijpstra sipped and looked at the two younger men.

"You know," he said thoughtfully, "we aren't doing very well."

"No?" de Gier asked.

"No, and I'll tell you why. First of all we have the Cat," Grijpstra said, "or, rather, we don't have him. He is still in our hands but we'll have to let him go tomorrow unless we can explain ourselves better. The public prosecutor won't let us hold him on that half-shaved mustache. We can't really prove he was on the run when we caught him and he has been very calm and self-possessed ever since we arrested him."

"You've got nothing else on him?" Cardozo asked.

Grijpstra, who was about to plunge into a long sentence, interrupted himself and looked at the young man.

"Are you on this case now, Cardozo?"

"I was on the young girl's death," Cardozo said. "The girl they found in the park. But everybody seems to think she gave herself an overdose and the case is closed now."

"What do *you* think?" de Gier asked.

"I don't think much."

"So you have nothing to do, have you?" Grijpstra asked. "Have you been detailed to us?"

"The commissaris mentioned I might come see you."

"All right, all right," Grijpstra said fiercely.

"We'll take you," de Gier said, "as long as you promise not to be in the way, and to do as you are told, and not to speak unless spoken to and . . ."

"I promise," Cardozo said.

"Right," Grijpstra said. "You asked a question just now. Here is the answer. We have nothing else on the Cat. A half mustache and a lot of thoughts, our thoughts. And the Mouse. You know about the Mouse?"

"I read the report," Cardozo said. "The commissaris let

me look through his file. I have just come from his office. And the chief inspector stopped me in the corridor and asked me to ask you to make less noise."

"We aren't making any noise," Grijpstra said. "We checked the Cat's warehouse and it is full of all sorts of goods. We checked through his books and he bought the goods all right. He is allowed to buy goods for resale since he is a merchant and owns a registered business. There are no TV sets in his warehouse, no washing machines, no paints, no building materials, nothing the Mouse mentioned. The Cat is still in the clear."

"Another warehouse," Cardozo suggested.

"Maybe, but where? Perhaps he stored the goods in the houses of the thieves. We found plenty on the dike, enough to keep all the other suspects in custody even if they weren't caught with firearms in their hands."

"Right," de Gier said, "that's bad. But we'll go into it today. What else is bad?"

"The man the motorcycle-sergeant shot; he is dying, I believe. He was operated on and the wound seemed all right but he is much worse now. That's bad for all of us. We aren't supposed to kill people; we're supposed to protect them against themselves."

"Hell," Cardozo said, "they were shooting at us with a tommy gun, weren't they? And that sergeant was tired. He had been up all night. I know him; he is a careful man. I am sure he aimed for the fellow's legs."

"OK," de Gier said, "that's bad too. What else?"

"Wernekink," Grijpstra shouted and jumped up. "He is dead, and he goes on being dead and nobody knows who did it except the killer."

De Gier sighed.

"And the case is geting old."

Cardozo was listening and nodding his head at the same time.

"Stop nodding," Grijpstra said. "You look silly when you nod. And you irritate me. We are supposed to work together, not irritate each other."

"He bought the coffee, didn't he?" de Gier asked.

"Sure, sure. But he shouldn't nod. You don't want him to nod either, do you?"

"Stop nodding, Cardozo," de Gier said.

Cardozo got up. He looked very pleasant and obedient. "I'll go do some work. What would you like me to do, adjutant?"

Grijpstra said nothing. "Find that second warehouse," de Gier said. "The Mouse never mentioned another warehouse but it's got to be somewhere. They were hijacking container-loads of goods, too much to store in those small houses on the dike."

"No," Grijpstra said, "I don't agree. And I don't want Cardozo to run about all day for nothing. I think they *did* store the goods on the dike. The Cat is intelligent, he wouldn't risk too much carting about. I think they took their goods to the dike in the early morning, stored them in and under their houses—they all have cellars and we did find goods in the cellars—and then took it straight to the addresses the Cat gave them. They had a small truck and they also had the cruiser on the river. I think the Cat only has one ware-house—the one he showed us—and there was nothing there."

"You talked to the Cat before he was arrested, didn't you?" Cardozo asked de Gier.

"Yes."

"Where?"

"It is in my report," de Gier said. "You read it."

"Sharif Electric," Grijpstra shouted and jumped up. "Clever Cardozo! Brilliant Cardozo! Excellent Cardozo!"

"Darling Cardozo," de Gier said.

Cardozo smiled.

"Electric," Grijpstra shouted, "Sharif Electric. And they were stealing electric household appliances. Who is Sharif?"

"I know," de Gier said.

"Tell us!"

"Sharif is the owner of a chain of discount stores. He sells electric household appliances. You have to pay cash but his prices are very low. He also sells camping goods and boats."

Grijpstra was listening intently.

"Don't know him personally," he said slowly. "I know his name now; I think I bought a sleeping bag in one of his stores once. For my son. Birthday present. A store near the central station, is that right?"

"Yes," de Gier said, "that's his main store, but he has others in the city and some in Rotterdam and The Hague and in the country too, I believe."

"Sharif, what sort of a name is that?"

"Arab," Cardozo said. "I know his full name. Mehemed el Sharif. He is rich and he owns a beautiful villa in New South with a garden on the river. I've been there once."

"Why? Do we have anything on him?"

"No. The place was burglarized while Sharif and his family were away. The thieves escaped with carpets and silverware and some other valuables but they couldn't break the safe. I saw Sharif when he came back from his trip. He wasn't very upset; everything was insured. He was worried about his cat, I remember. He had left the cat in the house and the neighbors were supposed to feed it. They had a key.

He thought that the burglars might have frightened the cat away. But the cat came back again."

"Good," de Gier said.

"Did we catch the thieves?"

"Yes, adjutant. Later. They were caught while they were breaking into another house and they confessed to a string of burglaries. We found some of the goods too and they were returned to Sharif."

"Neighbors had nothing to do with it?"

"No."

"What was he like, this Sharif fellow?"

"A tall handsome man with a beard. He wore an Arab dress—a burnoose, I think they call it—when I went to see him at his house."

"Nice fellow?"

"I think so. Soft-spoken and quiet. He gave me some strong coffee in a small cup and I sat on the floor. An exciting house too, beautifully furnished. Carpets everywhere. He had to pray in the middle of our conversation. They have set times for prayer, you know. Got himself a small carpet and started bowing down and getting up and mumbling to himself. Beautiful!"

"That's nice," de Gier said.

"Wife? Family?" Grijpstra asked.

"An Arab wife who doesn't speak Dutch and two children, small children."

"Does Sharif speak Dutch?"

"Fluently."

"How long has he been here?"

"I asked him. He came after the war. First guest laborer into the country he said. Made a joke about it. He said he really came as a guest, not as a laborer. Said he didn't like to work."

Grijpstra turned to de Gier. "Didn't you say in your report that the Cat was buying used carpet tiles from him and had bought them because Sharif had no further use for them? They'd been used at an exhibition or something?"

"Yes. I found the carpet tiles in the Cat's warehouse. He meant to sell them to the street market at double the price he paid. It was a big deal, he said, close to six thousand guilders."

Grijpstra had picked up the phone and was dialing the commissaris' number. The conversation didn't take long. "He is coming down," Grijpstra said. "Good work, Cardozo. We need a fresh brain. De Gier is getting fat and I am getting old; we can't see what is staring us in the face."

De Gier jumped up. "Fat?"

"I am fatter maybe," Grijpstra said, "but the fat is all over me. Nicely divided. But you have it all in one place. There." He poked de Gier in the stomach.

"I can't see it," Cardozo said.

"Breathe out, de Gier," Grijpstra said. "You see? There it is. A lump. A sort of ball. It's the fried noodles and all that other starch he eats. Should eat apples and do some judo practice."

De Gier was getting red in the face. "I practice twice . . ."

"Gentlemen," the commissaris said.

The conversation took well over an hour but they finally agreed. They wouldn't be able to find the connection with the Cat and most of his helpers in jail, but they might find something if they worked from Sharif's side.

"If he received the goods," the commissaris said, "he must have paid with black money. There can't be any invoices in his bookkeeping. But the appliances must be in his shops, so that's where we should look. It may explain Sharif Electric's low prices. Suppose he has a hundred TV sets, fifty are bought officially at the right price and fifty come from the Cat at half-price. His average buying price is seventy-five percent of normal value. He adds a profit of fifty or sixty percent—whatever he can ask in his trade—and he makes more money than his competitors while he is selling at approximately twenty-five percent below their prices."

De Gier, whose comprehension of abstract figures was low, had closed his eyes.

"You follow, de Gier?"

De Gier opened his eyes. "Yes, sir. Who is going to check the records of his stores? Sharif probably keeps his stock records and invoices at his central office, the warehouse where I met the Cat for the first time. Somebody ought to go there while others are checking the shops."

"Not you three," the commissaris said. "We have specialists. I'll go talk to their chief now and see if they can start right away. We may be too late as it is. Sharif knows what is going on as well as we do and he may have ordered his employees to take the stolen appliances out."

"We should be able to catch him," Grijpstra said. "He has a number of shops and to shift all that stuff around would be an effort involving a lot of people. One of them will talk, especially when it is suggested to them that they may be in trouble themselves if they pretend to know nothing."

"What do *we* do, sir?" de Gier asked.

"Grijpstra should go talk to Sharif himself I think, and you and Cardozo can snoop about. Start at his house and check his file at the aliens department. He isn't a Dutch citizen now, is he, Cardozo?"

"No, sir; he has an Egyptian passport. He told me when

I was at his house. But he has had a resident's permit for years and years."

"We may have some information on him," the commissaris said. "Good luck. Let me know if you find something. I may be at home but you have my number."

Grijpstra arrived at Sharif Electric's head office at the same time as the detectives of the commercial investigation department. There were two of them and the three policemen trooped into the Arab's office.

Their host was graceful, and calm. He asked the policemen to sit down while he read the warrant. He telephoned his bookkeeper and gave permission to show the files. The bookkeeper came and asked the two detectives to follow him.

"Well, adjutant," Sharif said pleasantly, "may I ask why this investigation is taking place?"

Grijpstra didn't feel at ease. The calm face of the Arab, the thin well-cared-for beard, and the hands—long and slender—lying quietly on the desk, unnerved him.

He waited, trying to find the right words.

Sharif waited with him.

"Well, sir," Grijpstra said at last, "there have been some irregularities recently. A lot of electric household goods have been stolen. Trucks have been hijacked, in Amsterdam and in the country, and in Belgium and West Germany as well. So far we haven't been able to trace the goods but we now have reason to believe that there may be a connection with your organization. Some of these goods may be, or may have been, in your stores."

The Arab smiled.

"Adjutant, the man you are now facing is a foreigner in your country, a guest. The Dutch have been my hosts since

1949, when I came here with little capital. I have been treated well and I am grateful. The Dutch have given me a chance to make a living and I have prospered. I own nine shops, apart from the building you are in now, and I deal in a number of commodities. In a way I have become a link between this country and the Arab world. In the twenty-six years that you have allowed me to live here I have never been in contact with the police. I have never even received a traffic ticket. My taxes have always been paid promptly. I am well known to all the ambassadors of the countries which speak my language and I know several members of your government. You have a warrant, and you have a right to be here. You are my guest, adjutant. But I do believe that a mistake has been made."

Grijpstra was silent.

The Arab allowed the silence to last a full minute.

"Perhaps," he said slowly, "I should ask you to reconsider your investigation. Here is a telephone. Would you like to contact your chief?"

Grijpstra took a deep breath.

"No, sir. The investigation will continue until we are satisfied."

"You are acting under orders, adjutant. I understand your position."

"Not quite, sir."

"You are not quite acting under orders?" the Arab asked and raised his eyebrows.

"I am Dutch," Grijpstra said in his normal booming voice. "The Dutch do not like to work under orders. It is true that I was asked to come here but I was not ordered. I came here because I thought the suggestion was right. We have reason to believe that there is a connection between the stolen goods and your organization, as I have already told you. Perhaps we are wrong. If we are we will apologize for the inconvenience caused and leave immediately."

The Arab smiled and picked up his telephone.

"Coffee, adjutant?"

"Please."

"Two coffees, please," Sharif said and replaced the hook, very gently, as if it might break.

He smiled. "Yes," he said, "I should know the Dutch a little. I admit that I have used the wrong word. I have worked with the Dutch for so long but I still translate from my own language when I try to say something. I never order my staff for they will put their hands in their pockets and glare at me. I invite them to do things. I understand now that you have been invited to come here. Very well, adjutant. Is there anything you want to ask me?"

The coffee gave Grijpstra a chance to think of the right answer, or the right questions, but he couldn't find any. He could only think of asking Sharif whether he had, indeed, bought stolen goods, but he didn't think there was any point in a blunt approach.

"Mr. Diets," he said in the end, "or the Cat as some people call him, do you know this man well, Mr. Sharif?"

"The Cat," Sharif said, "is known to me, but it is very difficult to know a man well. The Cat acts a part and he is a good actor. A conscious actor. We are all actors, of course, but we don't always know we are acting. We wear masks, even if we think we are being open and straightforward. Sometimes I wonder what is under the masks. Do you know, adjutant?"

Grijpstra replaced his coffee cup as gently as Sharif had replaced the telephone. He looked at Sharif and his face was set.

"I don't think you know, adjutant," Sharif continued,

"and neither do I. But I wonder sometimes. I have wondered, in fact, if there is anything at all under these masks. We put them on at birth, and perhaps they are taken away when we die. It's a frightening thought, don't you think, that there may be *nothing* under the masks."

"Mr. Diets," Grijpstra said, "the Cat."

"Yes. I haven't forgotten your question. I like to wander a bit at times; it helps to find the truth. There must be truth. And we must be able to find it. The Prophet found it and the Prophet was a man, not a god. I have thought that I have seen glimpses of the truth but when I try to remember them they escape me. It makes me happy and sad at the same time."

Grijpstra shuddered.

"Are you cold, adjutant? Shall I open the windows? The sun will be getting hot soon. It's nearly eleven o'clock now, and it has almost reached this room. In a minute it will be with us."

"I am all right, sir."

"Or did you shudder at what I said? You are a man like I am a man, adjutant. We live on the same planet and our circumstances do not differ in essence. Perhaps you are touched by what I was saying. We both have our dreams, perhaps our dreams met just now."

Damn, Grijpstra thought, damn, *damn*! I am getting too much of this lately. He is right. There was the sound of that cucumber this morning. The sound touched me. It made me talk about the dream I have, the dream that slips away. Now this. What? *What?*

"Mr. Diets," the Arab's soft voice was saying, "he buys carpet tiles from me, very cheaply. He is smart. He resells them to the street market and makes a good profit. He has brought other things from me. I told you I deal in various commodities. I buy secondhand clothes and export them to Africa. I import aromatic oils. I have several regular lines. But sometimes I find odd goods and I buy them because I think I may be able to sell them again, but I make mistakes. When I make a mistake Mr. Diets, the Cat as you and I call him, comes and buys. The transactions are not always recorded in my books. Cash money changes hands and the deal is forgotten. I believe the government chooses not to notice such deals. The street markets have a function; they keep prices down. If the street markets are checked too carefully and the tax rules are applied too stringently the markets will wither. They will disappear in the end. That wouldn't be good for the country."

"I am a police detective, sir," Grijpstra said happily, glad to be back on familiar ground. "If you pay or receive black money the tax inspectors will be interested. The tax department has its own detectives."

"Yes. You mentioned stolen goods."

"Yes, sir."

"I have not bought stolen goods. I have not sold them."

Grijpstra got up. "Very well, sir."

De Gier and Cardozo were looking at the house.

"What now?" Cardozo asked.

"There it is," de Gier said. "Nice house!"

"Nice house! That house is worth three or four hundred thousand guilders. It has a garden like a park, it's three stories high, it must have twenty or more rooms, and the garage is big enough for four cars."

"There are dozens of houses like that in Amsterdam," de Gier said.

Cardozo snarled.

"You don't approve of rich people?"

"Property is theft," Cardozo said firmly.

De Gier sighed. "Another communist. Grijpstra says the same thing."

"Don't you agree?"

"No," de Gier said firmly, "I don't agree and I don't disagree. I don't care!"

Cardozo turned round. "You really don't care?"

"No."

"What do you care about?"

"Nothing," de Gier said. "No. I care about my cat. But if he dies, he dies. I care about him as long as he is there."

"Nothing else?"

"No."

"Wernekink's death?"

"No," de Gier said. "I don't care about Wernekink's death."

"You don't want to find out who got him?"

"Of course I want to find out," de Gier said. "Why do you think I'm here? Wernekink knew the Cat and the Cat has some connection with Sharif and Sharif lives in this house. And goods have been stolen. So I'm here, admiring the house."

Cardozo scratched about in his thick hair. "I'm supposed to be intelligent, sergeant, but I don't follow you."

"I don't care if you follow me or not," de Gier said, "but we may as well go away. We can't snoop around in the garden; it has a sign 'beware of dogs' and we would be trespassing anyway. There are no shops around except the supermarket in the next block and I am not going to ask them if they know Sharif, for they won't. I'm going to have lunch. Coming?"

"Yes, yes," Cardozo said, "but there must be a way. He must have friends, habits, places he goes to. Is there an

Arab club in town? Arab cafés? Arabs don't drink liquor, I believe."

"They are not supposed to," de Gier said, "but Amsterdam is the place where you do what you aren't supposed to do."

"As long as you don't cause too much trouble," Cardozo said.

"Yes. Tell you what we'll do. We'll get a list of all Arab places in town from the aliens department or from somewhere else. The aliens people haven't been too helpful. They said they had nothing on Sharif. I often suspect them of trying to protect their charges."

"So they should."

"Sure, sure. Stop interrupting. We get a list and we split it. You take half, or a third if Grijpstra wants to join in. But we won't go anywhere until seven tonight. Then we'll meet on the Dam square at ten P.M., near the lion on the north side of that horrible big penis sticking up in the middle. And now we eat. In a Chinese restaurant. Fried noodles. You pay, Cardozo."

"Why me?" Cardozo asked. "I payed for the coffee this morning. It's your turn."

"No," de Gier said, "I'm really hungry and when I'm really hungry, you pay. You're younger."

"Does the adjutant make you pay when he is really hungry?"

"Always. There's a streetcar. Let's catch it."

"OK. I'll pay. It'll be a pleasure."

They ran but the streetcar driver was too fast for them and the automatic doors closed just as they reached the tram stop.

"Did you say 'pleasure'?" de Gier asked.

"Yes."

"When you say 'pleasure' you should try to look pleasant. Try again."

Cardozo tried.

"Not bad," de Gier said, "but it could be better. You need practice."

"No," Cardozo said softly, "no, no, no."

"Pardon?" de Gier asked but Cardozo was trying to read his neighbor's newspaper.

"Go away," the man said. "I hate waiting at tram stops and I hate holding a newspaper with the wind blowing, and I detest other people trying to read my newspaper. Buy your own."

"No money," Cardozo said.

"Then go beg."

"Have you got fifty cents, please?" Cardozo whined. "Please, sir?"

"No," the man said.

IT WAS THREE-THIRTY THAT SAME AFTERNOON AND THE commissaris, who had left Headquarters early after having reported sick but still available for urgent matters, felt the temperature of his bath. The pain in his legs had been building up all morning until he felt that he would faint or scream out. He knew, by bitter experience, that only a very hot bath would ease the pain and now the moment was close. He felt the water again and the temperature was right. The water was very hot. He lowered his body gradually and sighed with relief. The pain was oozing away. He was completely detached from anything now. He no longer knew who he was. And at that exact moment of almost complete liberation he knew that Tom Wernekink had been killed by mistake, had been taken for someone else.

* * *

De Gier agreed two hours later. He had got his list of Arab meeting places in town and reported at the adjutant's desk. Grijpstra approved the plan and regretted he couldn't join his two assistants. He had promised Mrs. Grijpstra to accompany her to her sister's birthday party.

"You don't want to go to a birthday party, do you?" de Gier asked.

"No."

"So why go?"

Grijpstra had waved him out of the room.

"Come with us," de Gier said at the door; "you'll like it. We can have a drink somewhere afterward."

Grijpstra went on waving.

And now de Gier was at home, walking about in a kimono with Oliver in his arms. Oliver purred.

"Silly cat," de Gier said and squeezed the Siamese. Oliver yelled but didn't try to wrestle himself out of de Gier's grip. De Gier squeezed again and Oliver reached out and placed a paw on de Gier's nose.

"We'll sleep for a while," de Gier said and stretched out on the large antique hospital bed that occupied two-thirds of his small bedroom. He released the cat, which jumped on his stomach, felt about for a good position and became limp. De Gier smiled and reached for the bars at the foot of the bed. His toes curled round the thin brass rods and he stretched his body, grunting with pleasure.

"This is it," he said to Oliver, who was watching him. "This is it, Oliver. You know I said today that I only care about you?" Oliver moved his ears. "Don't pretend you're listening. You don't have to listen to words. You understand. More than I do probably, but in a way I can't learn. I said I only cared about you, but it isn't true. There is something

I care about but I can't reach it, like Grijpstra can't reach his dream."

De Gier's eyes were closing. Sleep hadn't yet come but he wasn't awake either. His own strength of concentration was being reinforced with whatever the cat was contributing. And then de Gier also knew that Tom Wernekink's death was a mistake. The riddle had been in his mind for some time now and the answer popped. A mistake.

And Grijpstra agreed as well. There was nothing about Grijpstra's condition at the time that could have been called special. He was in his office, behind his desk, reading through a list of stolen motorized bicycles. His mind wasn't registering any of the makes or numbers. There was a drumstick in his right hand and he was touching the smallest drum with it, without making much of a sound.

"A mistake," Grijpstra said softly. "He thought he was killing somebody else—somebody important—somebody who was upsetting his plans. The man was mixed up, caught in a scheme."

He banged a little louder now.

"A scheme. What sort of a scheme? Something to do with the dike, of course, with the hijacking and the stealing and the receiving."

"Elise," the commissaris called.

"Yes, dear?"

His wife was standing next to the bath, bowing down to him.

"How is the pain now, dear?"

"It has gone, Elise. Would you mind . . ."

"Yes, dear," his wife smiled and left the bathroom. She was back in a minute with a tray. There was a big glass of orange juice with ice cubes floating in it on the tray, and an ashtray, a tin of cigars and a box of matches. She took a cigar and lit it, trying to keep the smoke out of her mouth, puffing it away.

"Shame," the commissaris said. "You don't have to do that you know. You can put the cigar in my mouth and light it for me."

"No, it might get wet. And I like doing things for you; it's only that I don't like the taste. Cigarettes aren't so bad. Here."

She put the cigar between his thin lips and left the tray on a stool.

"I've got some coffee going. I'll bring it when it is ready."

"Yes, dear."

I've got it, the commissaris thought. Something anyway. It's the old trick, the trick of the clever leader. He smiled, and the cigar moved and nearly fell into the hot water. It's the trick I use myself sometimes. I'll say, "Certainly, I will mention your idea to the chief constable," and then I will say later, "Ah, yes, I suggested your idea to the chief constable, but he isn't in favor, not just now."

He reached out and took hold of the glass of orange juice. But I would never have spoken to the chief constable. It's always good to create an obstacle, an obstacle they can't reach themselves. That's what the Cat must have done. Somebody must have suggested something to him. He couldn't say no straight out but he wasn't going to do what they wanted him to do either. So he stalled them and said he would ask his boss. In the Cat's case the method was even better than what I try to do sometimes. The detectives know the chief constable but they'll never ask him anything directly; they go through us, their immediate superiors. But the Cat invented a boss. He didn't tell anyone who the boss was. He said he would ask the boss, but there was no boss. And then later he would say that the boss wasn't in favor, not just now.

"Thank you, dear," the commissaris said and his wife put the cup on the tray and left.

The commissaris sat up, put the empty glass back and started on his coffee. He continued thinking. So they got tough. They shadowed the Cat and found out that he was always visiting Tom Wernekink. They say Wernekink's posh sports car and they must have looked through the windows and seen his wealth inside. A very rich man with no occupation. And the Cat goes to see him all the time. They wanted something of the Cat. They probably wanted him to join them, to give in somehow, to drop part of his profits by lowering his prices. The Cat was stalling them and he was still too strong to tackle. So they decided to shock him.

The commissaris twisted his toe around the hot-water tap and shifted his legs so that he wouldn't get burned by the sudden stream of steaming water. He shifted his body and the warmth spread right into his bones. There was no pain now but he didn't feel his usual contentment that began to glow immediately after the pain ceased. He felt dread, the dread that the Cat must have felt when he heard about Tom Wernekink's death. They had wanted him to feel dread, not just fear. They had wanted him to wake up to the horrifying implications of their conduct. They wanted the Cat to know that they were prepared to kill a man on incomplete evidence.

The commissaris maneuvered his foot and the hot-water tap closed again. He lit another small cigar after drying his hands carefully with the towel his wife had left on the floor.

* * *

Yes, de Gier thought on his way to the kitchen. He had slept and now it was time to eat. Soon he would be going to town to meet Cardozo. Wernekink was killed by mistake. They figured it all wrong, the bastards. They merely *thought* that Wernekink might be connected with the gang on the dike. They never bothered to prove their theory. Perhaps they didn't even care. But whose mind constructed this bit of terrorism? They wanted to get at the Cat, of course, but they killed his friend. His friend was of no use to them. He had no active part in the gang. They needed the Cat, but they needed a scared Cat, not a confident Cat.

Maybe it was my friend Sharif, Grijpstra thought as he was dressing in front of his small bathroom mirror. My friend Sharif, the wise man from the East. The man who has become a millionaire in a foreign country by selling stolen household appliances at a twenty-five percent discount, importing aromatic oils, and exporting secondhand clothes to the blacks in Africa.

He brushed his short hair and patted the bald spot, which the hairs, no matter which way he brushed them, would no longer hide. Fat, old and bald, Grijpstra said to his image, and stupid. Can you imagine Sharif creeping about in Wernekink's river garden, aiming, firing a pistol, and sneaking out again?

He saw the smooth gentleman again, with the large, almost liquid, eyes. Grijpstra shuddered, as he had shuddered in Sharif's office that day. "What's under the mask, adjutant? I don't think you know. Neither do I. We are both men, we both live on the same planet. We have the same questions. You have a dream that escapes you, yet it seems within reach. The Prophet had the dream, and he was a man like us, adjutant."

Would a man like that, a man who could read Grijpstra's dream, whose eyes were so soft and deep and whose hands were so long and slender and quiet, kill Tom Wernekink— a harmless eccentric—just for the hell of it? Just to shake another man who might be of use to him in a scheme of mere material profit? Grijpstra thought.

Some forgotten knowledge surfaced in Grijpstra's mind. Infidels, he thought, that's what we are in their minds. Their faith is deep but it is pushed on others. They are prepared to draw a sword, to point a pistol, only to convince. They will kill if the infidel refuses to be convinced. To kill is nothing to them; it's still a sport, a gesture. Embrace the faith or lose your head.

He tried to brush his hair the other way but the bald spot was still there. But that's the faith, he said to his uncooperative image, and the faith is not a washing machine, or a twenty-five percent profit. Hadn't Sharif said to him, only a few hours ago, "Adjutant, we are both men"? Would Sharif the philosopher be prepared to put a bullet into Grijpstra's large heavy head if he, Grijpstra, frustrated a deal in used clothes?

He didn't know the answer to his question and shook his head helplessly. His body had filled itself with submerged nausea. The incongruity of the case made him feel as if he were walking in a desert of twilight.

Apply for a transfer to some small city, he told himself. Amsterdam is too subtle for you. What do you know about Arabs? Or Chinese?

He sighed. What do you know about the Dutch? he asked himself and knotted his tie and stamped into the corridor where his wife was shouting for him.

"Yes," he shouted back. "I *am* coming. And if your damned brother-in-law is going to switch the TV on I am going to drink all beer in the house and you can carry me home."

"I won't," his wife shouted.

"You will," he said. "Oh yes, you will, because if you don't you'll have no one to shout at tomorrow morning."

〰〰 12 〰〰

TEN O'CLOCK ON A SUMMER NIGHT IN AMSTERDAM. SUM-
mer was creeping into autumn but the hot heavy weather
held on and the city was limp after an exhausting day. The
terraces had been full and the shops empty. Girls had displayed their crossed legs on the metal or cane chairs of the
terraces but the men had been too sweaty and irritable to
show much interest. Even the mini skirts that showed all,
the belly buttons that accentuated naked waists decorated
with thin golden chains, even the pink, brown, yellow and
black breasts pushed up cleverly by invisible plastic struc-
tures had failed to raise more than a quick glance. The
newspapers bought out of habit remained unread, left on
the tables of cafés and on the seats of streetcars and buses.
There had been no queues at the cinemas, and theaters and
concert halls were empty that night. Only beer trucks and
Italian ice carts were busy. The water in the canals was

green and stagnant and the pigeons on the Dam square only moved when a human foot almost crushed them. Even then they didn't bother to fly away but only moved over with an angry or merely disturbed "korroo, korroo."

De Gier leaned against the pedestal of the Northern Lion, an unlikely looking stone animal. Together with its mate, the Southern Lion, it had been built by a well-meaning architect who had designed the immense white concrete phallus pointing at heaven to remind everyone that the War had been terrible and had taken many Dutch lives. The gray steps surrounding the phallus were crowded, as ever, with sweet-eyed hippies, leather-jacketed drug dealers and mentally deranged youngsters who were hugging each other for company. Several guitars clanged in sad disharmony and some elegant black beauties were talking to each other in the dialect of Surinam, the last Dutch colony on the South American continent. Now threatened by independence, it was losing its population in a steady trickle via Schiphol airport at the rate of at least one full four-engined jet plane a day. Dutch welfare provided these young people with their bell-bottomed trousers, striped shirts and high-heeled boots. And here they were in the shadow of the phallus enjoying their sudden freedom from the claws of hunger and disease, trying to get used to a new environment that, so far, showed few signs of accepting them. De Gier had been looking at them for some time, the great-great-great-grandchildren of slaves taken some hundreds of years ago by Arab and Dutch vessels from the west coast of Africa to the new promising colony of sugar and cotton fields—slaves who died like rats on ships and plantations but who were always replaced by fresh deliveries. De Gier sighed.

Two drug dealers ambled up to him. They didn't look

at him but their lips moved. "Hashshshshshshshsh. Hashshshshshshshsh."

The hissing sounded uncanny and vaguely threatening. The dealers were young, wide-shouldered and long-haired. Evil yogis, perverted fakirs with black souls full of hatred and greed and spite.

"Fuck offffffffff, fuck offffffffff," de Gier hissed.

The dealers turned and came straight for him. A blue VW bus, parked at the curb, showed a ripple of interest. The three uniformed constables in the bus had been watching the dealers; they now sat up, ready to slide their door open. De Gier's body moved too. He stood with his legs apart, his arms dangling. His chin was down. He had already worked out his attack. A quick feint to the one on the left and a kick in the shins to the one on the right that would floor the young man and put him out of the fight for a few seconds. Then he would hit the one on the left with a backhanded slap and punch him full in the stomach. Turning again toward the one on the right, who should have been on his feet by that time, practicing the best possible judo throw, de Gier would jump, put his right foot against the man's chest, grab him by the shoulders, fall back and propel the body over his head. The man might break his neck if he didn't know how to fall but de Gier wasn't concerned. The sympathy of the nation would be with him. There was no way to catch these ghouls. They carried no drugs or proper weapons. They might use a screwdriver or a paint scraper, arms that kill if they don't maim and are legal as long as they aren't used in actual violence. If he followed them they would walk him to a parked car, or a hole in a wall and sell him drugs. They might also rob him.

Go on, de Gier thought, attack me. Please.

But the dealers spat at him and changed direction. They

had seen the constables in the bus. They had also seen the way de Gier was waiting for them. They wouldn't attack. They only went for the weak, the helpless, the hopeless. De Gier looked at his watch. Five past ten. No Cardozo. A throng of hippies passed, chanting a song of love. When they thinned out he saw Cardozo, leaning against the pedestal of the Southern Lion.

De Gier walked over and approached Cardozo from the back, making no sound on his thick rubber soles. Cardozo turned around just before de Gier's hand touched his shoulder. Cardozo was also ready, legs apart, arms dangling.

"It's you," Cardozo said; "you're late. Funny atmosphere here this evening, don't you think? There'll be a fight soon I bet. The dealers are wandering about everywhere and they seem nastier than usual. I've had a few girls making up to me as well; heroin must be in very short supply all of a sudden. When they raise the price the activity increases immediately. They'll be busier than usual at the station tonight."

"I am not late," de Gier said, "you're in the wrong place. This is the Southern Lion, we were supposed to meet at the Northern Lion."

Cardozo smiled. "Sorry, sergeant. I never knew the difference."

"There is south," de Gier said, pointing, "and there's the north. Direction of the Central Station. Didn't they ever make you find your way during the exercises at the police school?"

"They did," Cardozo said, "the works. They have dumped me from a moving truck right in the middle of nowhere."

"So what happened? Did they pick you up in the forest a couple of days later? Wandering about in a daze?"

"No," Cardozo said.

"So?"

"I always carried some money," Cardozo said, "and there are five hundred Dutchmen to the square kilometer. I could always ask, couldn't I?"

"You shouldn't have asked and you shouldn't have carried money."

"Should," Cardozo said.

"Every man has his weaknesses," de Gier said. "You'll find out about mine if you live long enough. How did it go with the Arabs?"

"Nothing," Cardozo said. "I have nothing. Do you have anything?"

De Gier shook his head. "Let's go. They're starting another song about love over there and there's another lot of dealers coming our way. If we keep on hanging about, the constables will arrest us for loitering. We stick out like blue herons in a crowd of ducks."

Cardozo giggled. "They wouldn't arrest us. They know me. Two of them were at the police school with me. And I am not exactly a heron. You perhaps, especially in that blue denim suit. I look more like a bittern."

"A bittern?" de Gier asked. "Aren't they the small fat birds that explode every now and then? You never see them but you hear them booming away in the marshlands. I heard one a few weeks ago when we were trying to locate a stolen river cruiser."

"They're ugly birds," Cardozo said.

"Nature is never ugly," de Gier said. "So you had no luck with the Arabs?"

Cardozo burped. "I ate something," Cardozo said. "Couscous they call it. It looks like brown semolina pudding and it's hot. They serve it with meat. It's still sitting in my stomach."

"And Sharif?"

"They ran for the phone when I mentioned his name. I only mentioned it twice—in a Moroccan eating place and in a Lybian coffeehouse. They claimed they had never heard the name but in both instances I saw a man sneak to the telephone."

"Yes," de Gier said thoughtfully, "the same happened to me. Only I didn't eat couscous. They gave me a bit of goat's leg with hairs on it and a half-cooked green pepper. I have eaten in Arab places before and the food was delicious. But this time I was treated like the enemy. Sharif must be a holy name to them—a head man who protects them—an idol perhaps. He became a millionaire and he has a white Lincoln and a driver. I think he is their self-respect."

"And if it is hurt they'll gang up on us?"

"They won't say anything," de Gier said. "They said nothing to you; they said nothing to me. A lot of them are illegal immigrants without any security. When we catch them we fly them straight back to wherever they came from. But sometimes they get help—someone pays a deposit for them while they apply for a visa. Sharif has a lot of money and he is a devout Moslem."

"So we can't catch him?"

De Gier suddenly stopped. They were in an alley behind the Dam square; it was a narrow alley and there wasn't much light. Cardozo bumped into him.

"Hey," Cardozo said.

"Of course we'll catch him," de Gier said. "We've had bad luck tonight but if we keep on trying we'll have good luck as well. Sharif has had good luck but his luck will change too."

"Tonight?" Cardozo asked.

"Tonight, or tomorrow night. Or next week some time."

"So what do we do now?"

"I have no idea," de Gier said, "but there's a pub on the next corner. I'll buy you a drink."

"No," Cardozo said. "I have paid for your coffee and I've paid for your lunch. Don't let me break the habit."

"All right," de Gier said. "If you insist."

De Gier stared moodily at his glass.

"Cheer up, sergeant. You remember about the good luck. It can come any moment now."

"Tell me a story," de Gier said, "anything, provided it is funny."

"Finish your drink, sergeant, and I'll buy you another one."

"Jenever isn't funny."

"I know a story," Cardozo said. "I told it to Adjutant Geurts once when we had a flat tire and were waiting for a truck to tow us away. The spare tire wasn't in the car and the adjutant was upset. The story made him laugh. Maybe it'll do something for you too."

De Gier raised his glass, drank its contents and held it up for more.

"Last month," Cardozo said, "there was a circus in town. They were parading the animals and the elephants were crossing a bridge. Traffic was congested as usual and a man in a VW was driving behind the last elephant, trying desperately to pass the cortege. He accelerated and turned his wheel but a truck was coming from the opposite direction and he had to go behind the elephant again. His foot slipped on the accelerator and the VW hit the elephant's hind leg. Being a circus elephant whose trainer had taught him that he should sit down if his hind leg was touched in a special way, the elephant sat down, right on the VW's nose."

"Ha," de Gier said.

"Yes. But the car was still usable. The man lives in Amsterdam North and he had to go through the big tunnel, the tunnel, so somebody told me, that you got yourself stuck in the other day. You had a lot of people with you and you ran out of petrol, didn't you? Right in the middle of the tunnel?"

"Yes," de Gier said.

"Pretty silly, wasn't it? Don't you check your petrol gauge before you drive off?"

"Yes, dear," de Gier said. "Go on with your funny story."

"OK. So the man drove into the tunnel but there was an accident just before he drove in and both lanes were stopped. The police arrived and were walking up and down, writing reports on the damaged cars. It was a chain collision and some twenty cars were damaged. When they got to his car they couldn't understand how it had got involved in the accident, since the car ahead and the car behind looked all right. But the VW was all crumpled up in front. They asked him what happened and he said an elephant had sat down on his hood."

"Ha."

"So they pulled him out of the car. They were pretty irritable already because of the heat and the noise in the tunnel and everybody running around shouting about their lovely cars all mucked up. And here was this boo-boo with his elephant joke. They put him on the back of a motorcycle, rushed him out of the tunnel and charged him with drunken driving. He had had a drink and smelled of alcohol."

"So?"

"It ended all right. When they took him to the station he kept on insisting that there had been an elephant and that it had sat on his car. They all laughed but finally a constable came who had seen the elephants in town. They phoned the circus and the man's story was confirmed."

De Gier laughed.

"Let's go," Cardozo said; "I've had three drinks and I usually begin to get drunk on the fourth. When I have the fourth I go on and on. I'll have a headache tomorrow."

"You want to go home?" de Gier asked.

"No. Let's look at the prostitutes for a while. There are some new ones around here. Some of these girls from Surinam are lovely. They are lit up by purple neon tubes and wear white lace."

They looked at the apparitions in the windows as they wandered about the red light district. They ate some meat rolls and drank coffee in a snackbar.

Cardozo pointed at a narrow high gabled house opposite the snackbar. "That house has always irritated me. It's been empty for years. We kept on warning the owner that the hippies would break into it, so they did of course and we couldn't get them out."

"That's the law," de Gier said. "Shortage of houses. It's the man's own fault."

"I know but it's a ridiculous law. The hippies were pushed out by the dealers and now it's a true hell hole. When I was still in uniform I helped raid the house a few times. We found children in there—shot full of heroin—old men sleeping in their own shit, fifteen-year-old prostitutes a week out of Surinam, and sacks full of imitation hash, and stolen goods and anything you can name."

"Let's have a look at it now," de Gier said.

They strolled over and saw a young girl standing in the door. They kept on walking.

"Listen," Cardozo said, "we have nothing to do anyway; let's do something. I'll go back alone and go in with the girl. One of my old mates was telling me that the house is used for robberies now. I think the girl is no prostitute but bait. In the clothes I'm wearing and with this bad haircut they may take me for a chappie from the country. I'll put it on, country accent and all. There may be some men in there who'll hold a knife to my throat and go for my wallet. Come in a few minutes later and we'll arrest the lot and take them to the station."

"OK," de Gier said, "but it's a big house; there may be a lot of people in it. I saw two plainclothes constables a minute ago; they're just wandering about too. Let's get them as well and go through the whole house."

They found the two constables, who grinned and said it was all right by them. They weren't supposed to do any raiding that night but if the sergeant suggested it . . .

"I suggest it," de Gier said, and took Cardozo's pistol and wallet.

Cardozo walked up to the house while de Gier and the two constables waited around a corner.

"Darling," the girl said.

Cardozo scratched his ear.

"Good evening."

"Come in. Twenty-five guilders. I'll strip naked for you and you do anything you like."

The girl was white, not yet twenty years old and dressed in a long skirt and white blouse with the top buttons undone. Her breasts were ripe and milky white. She stood so close to Cardozo that he could smell the mixture of sweat and perfume. She moved a little so that the split in her skirt opened and he could see her leg, right up to the top of her thigh. She put her hand on his shoulder and smiled. One of her front teeth was missing.

"I have more than twenty-five guilders," Cardozo said.

"How much?"

"A hundred."

"For a hundred you can stay all night. What would like me to do with you? Do you know any exciting tricks?"

"All right, I'll go with you," Cardozo stuttered.

"Come in, darling."

The men were waiting for him at the end of the corridor. One of them grabbed the small detective and hit him on the side of the head. It was a vicious blow that almost stunned him. He was pushed against the wall and a knife touched to his throat while hands quickly went through his pockets.

"Shit," a voice said. "He's got nothing on him. Nothing! What do you mean coming in here with nothing on you, monkey? You want us to cut your balls off?"

The knife now pressed against his throat with some force. Soon the skin would break.

"Police!" There were running feet in the corridor. The knife clattered to the floor as the ghoul pulled back and crumpled up. De Gier had hit him with the flat of his hand just under the ear. The constables were after the other man and caught him as he tried to reach the courtyard. The two men were handcuffed together and to a gas tube. De Gier pressed Cardozo's pistol into his hand and they ran up the stairs together.

All the doors of the rooms upstairs were open except one and de Gier kicked it with such force that the lock fell out of the rotten wood. The door, slamming back, hit the young man standing behind it and pushed him to the floor. The girl was cowering in a corner. Another man was trying to climb out the window and a third, holding a pistol, faced the two detectives rushing at him. He dropped the pistol just before Cardozo reached him. De Gier pulled the other man back from the window by the collar of his jacket and slammed him against the wall.

"Nice catch," the desk sergeant said twenty minutes later at the Warmoes Street police station. "Very nice. Five hoodlums, one female lure, five knives and one alarm pistol. Why all the energy, de Gier? You think we can't take care of our own district? The house was due to be raided anyway, you know."

"Sorry, sergeant," de Gier said. "We were getting upset about never having anything to do."

"No," the sergeant said. "Seriously, what caused all this; are you working on a special case?"

"Wernekink's death," de Gier said. "The dead body on the dike in North. The case connects up with your district, we think."

"Nobody ever tells us anything."

"No time. Do you mind if I interrogate one of the suspects? Your constables can do the reports but perhaps there is something in it for us."

"Sure."

"You're an Arab, aren't you?" de Gier asked the suspect, a short thickset man some thirty years old. The man was massaging his neck where de Gier had hit him during the arrest.

"Yes. Casablanca."

"Do you have a permit to stay in Holland?"

"No."

"How come you speak Dutch?"

"I have been here five years."

"Never caught before?"

"Yes. They flew me back two years ago."

"And you came straight back?"

The man smiled. "I was back before the military police who took me home got back to Schiphol airport. Came back on the next flight."

"You are in trouble now," de Gier said, "real trouble. You put a knife on a policeman's throat. Assault and robbery. And we'll get you for pimping as well. And drugs. There are detectives in the house now, tearing it apart. They'll find drugs, don't you think?"

"Maybe."

"You'll be in jail for a while, a long while."

The man's smile had gone. He was staring at the floor. "How long, sir? How long will I be in?"

De Gier gave the man a cigarette and lit it for him. They were in a small white-washed room, sitting in low easy chairs. Cardozo came in with three paper cups of coffee. A calendar on the wall opposite the window showed a color photograph of a forest.

"Don't know," de Gier said. "Two years, three maybe, depends on you and on the judge."

"Let me go," the man said. "I'll go and I won't come back this time, I promise. I haven't harmed him."

He pointed at Cardozo. Cardozo felt his throat.

"You almost did," Cardozo said. "You were pressing that knife, you miserable sod. How many times did you use that knife on some fool that girl sucked into the house?"

The man didn't answer.

"Well?" de Gier asked.

"A few times."

"There have been complaints about the house, you know. We can find the people who complained and each victim will provide a separate charge. More time in jail."

"Do you know a man called Sharif? Mehemed el Sharif?"

"Yes," the man said.

"What do you know about him?"

"Very rich, very important, very powerful."

"You work for him?"

"No."

"Tell us about him."

The man looked up. He was rubbing the side of his neck again.

"You want me to fall into the canal? What do you want to know? And what do you do if I tell you?"

"Where does he go at night? Who are his friends? Where do we find him when he is not at home and not in his office?"

"What will you do for me when I tell you?"

"I say," Cardozo said, "the other men we caught in the house, are they Arabs?"

"Dutch," the man said, "and Spanish—two Dutch, two Spanish."

"You're the only Arab, are you?"

"Yes."

"We'll forget about the knife," de Gier said, "and that's a big favor. We never saw a knife. This knife."

He was holding up a stiletto and pressed the button. The long thin blade shot out.

"That'll save you some time in jail."

"Forget everything," the man said, "and I'll tell you how to catch Sharif. And give me money; I'll need it. I can't stay in Holland and I can't go home. Sharif's arm is too long. I'll have to go to France and even in France I won't be safe."

"No," de Gier said. "We'll forget the knife, that's all. And Sharif will never know."

"He'll know. I won't tell."

"All right," de Gier said and got up.

"No," the man said. "Wait!"

De Gier and Cardozo waited. The man swallowed a few times. "There's a club, a brothel. There's some gambling too. Sharif doesn't own the club but he goes there once a week to meet some men who work for him. He'll be there tomorrow night, at ten o'clock. They talk in a special room. Then the men drink and play with the whores and gamble. Sharif doesn't drink but he plays with the women. He may stay until two o'clock."

"The address."

"Prince Alexander Street in South, number sixty-three; it's a big house. Members only."

"Did you ever meet him there?"

"No," the man said. "I won't say more. This is enough. If you tell Sharif I told you I am dead. Forget the knife and tell me your names. It's a bad deal for me. I give more than I get."

"Sergeant de Gier," de Gier said, "and Constable First-Class Cardozo. Headquarters. We'll forget the knife and lose it; it won't be in the report on you. Ask the sergeant to phone if you need us."

He got up and opened the door.

A constable came and took the Arab away with him. The Arab didn't look up. He was stumbling.

"He's scared," de Gier said, "really scared."

"So was I," Cardozo said, "when he had that knife on my throat. You took your time, didn't you. And he was breathing garlic at me as well."

"Yes," de Gier said. "I was telling the constables the story about your elephant. We laughed a lot and we almost forgot you."

||||| 13 |||||

"THEY AREN'T HERE, SIR," GRIJPSTRA SAID. "DE GIER phoned in this morning to say that he would arrive at eleven and Cardozo would also be late. They had some adventures last night, sir."

"What adventures?"

Grijpstra told him what he knew. De Gier's sleepy voice hadn't given him more than a general outline and Oliver, who hadn't been fed yet and was standing on de Gier's chest, yowled through the conversation.

"Hmm," the commissaris said; "it sounds promising anyway. When they come in I'd like to see all of you."

The three detectives looked worn out when they finally arrived in the commissaris' office at eleven-thirty. Grijpstra looked worse than the others. The birthday party at his sister-in-law's hadn't been a success. He had drunk his way through half a crate of beer while he watched funny men on the TV and listened to the political ideas of his brother-in-law. There had been a rip-roaring fight with his wife afterward, all the way home and another hour in the bedroom. And he had been sick. When it was all over and he finally reached his bed his wife had begun to snore and he got up again to look for his cigars. He stumbled and hurt his leg on the open door of the night table. The shin bled and the wound still worried him now. He was rubbing it.

"Pain in your legs, Grijpstra?" the commissaris asked, his voice betraying a more than usual interest.

"Hurt my shin, sir."

"But you weren't in the fight last night, were you?"

"No, sir. Door of the night table."

De Gier grinned. "How was the birthday party, Grijpstra?"

Grijpstra glared.

"Went to a party, Grijpstra?" the commissaris asked.

"Yes, sir, my sister-in-law's."

"Nice party?"

"No, sir."

The commissaris nodded. He had stopped going to parties ten years ago, when his rheumatism had begun to change from an occasional twitch of pain to a worsening and continuous feeling of hot needle pricks. He had never regretted his decision.

"I never go to birthday parties," de Gier said. "To hell with their birthdays and whipped cream cakes and lukewarm jenever. I'd rather have a quiet evening with Oliver."

"And you, Cardozo?" the commissaris asked.

"I'm from a big family, sir, and we are very close. I can't stay away."

"Do you ever want to stay away?"

"No, sir, not really. I get bored sometimes but I like my family and the food is always excellent."

"Good," the commissaris said. "The family is the core of our society. A happy family makes for a quiet country."

De Gier was looking at the old man's face. The commissaris looked sincere but de Gier didn't trust the innocent and genial expression on his superior's face.

"Well, let's have it," the commissaris said, rubbing his hands energetically. "What happened last night, de Gier?" De Gier reported fully and left out nothing except the confusion of the Northern and Southern Lions. The commissaris was leaning forward in his chair. "Good," he said at the end, "but we are going to have a little trouble with the chief inspector of the old city. I am sure he doesn't like us hunting in his territory. I'd better phone him before he phones me. I hope we didn't upset any of his plans. I know they are meaning to raid some of their trouble spots. Public Works should do something about that house, brick it up or get the restoration people on to it. Once it is repaired it can be let to decent people."

"Decent people don't like that area much, sir," Cardozo said.

"Yes. Maybe we should put some pressure on the city government. They have plans for a big state sex center somewhere, but so far they are only talking about it. It would make our job a lot easier. Put a high wall round it and post police at the entrances. Keep a lid on the kettle. But it's still too early for that."

"Would be a pity," Grijpstra said heavily.

"You like the whores' quarter, don't you?"

"It's been in the city for seven hundred years, sir. So far we have always been able to control it reasonably well."

"They do look pretty behind their windows," said de

Gier. "I can't imagine half-naked women in a concrete box, and behind barbed wire. Would be horrible."

"Yes, perhaps. Anyway, we'll wait and see. The police always wait and see. We are seeing something now. What are your plans, gentlemen?"

He was looking at Grijpstra.

Grijpstra cleared his throat and felt his pockets for his tin of cigars. The commissaris offered him one from the box on his desk. De Gier, with a show of servility, lit a match and Cardozo's young face brightened with a flashing smile as he concentrated on Grijpstra.

Grijpstra looked suspicious.

"Grrm, grrm, let's not overdo it," he muttered.

"Overdo what, adjutant?" de Gier asked. "We are listening."

"Yes," Grijpstra said. "Well, I think two of us should go to the brothel tonight, or one of us, while the other waits in the car. He should go to the doorman, show his police card and stay with him while he phones or calls the boss. Then he should take the boss to the car and tell him that we are after Sharif and that we know he will be there tonight. We can put in a bit about the illegal gambling and other illegal activities of the place so that the boss is quiet and helpful. Then we go in, pretending to be clients. We should be carrying money; the place won't be cheap and we don't want to be served free drinks."

"Yes," the commissaris said. "Who goes?"

"Not me," Grijpstra said. "Sharif knows me. And he may remember Cardozo's face since Cardozo went to see him last year about that burglary in his house. So I would suggest Geurts or Sietsema and de Gier."

"I think I would like to go," the commissaris said.

"That would be even better, sir. The clients of the place

won't be young men; there'll be older gentlemen and you would be just right."

"Thanks," the commissaris said. "Thank you kindly. I look like an old whoremonger, do I? Now that's really charming of you."

Grijpstra blushed and de Gier and Cardozo looked amused.

"Sorry, sir. I didn't mean that at all, sir."

The commissaris smiled. "Never mind, Grijpstra; I'm only joking. I think you're right. A place like that will attract people who look like me. Go on."

"So you and de Gier, sir. You'll be at the bar and you can look about. The boss will let you know when Sharif gets to the special room where he meets his men. Then you will have to find a place where you can listen in. Perhaps there is a peephole. Whorehouses always have peepholes, I believe. And you could use a tape recorder."

"Yes. We'll have to check that with the boss. Perhaps we can hide in a cupboard."

"What next, Grijpstra?"

"Depends on what they say. You may find Wernekink's killer too."

"That's de Gier's thought, isn't it? Didn't you tell me on the phone this morning that de Gier was thinking that Sharif or one of his men killed Wernekink?"

"Yes, sir."

The commissaris got up and walked around his desk. He leaned against the front of the desk and watched his assistants.

"I think de Gier is right. Wernekink's death must have been a silly mistake. But understandable perhaps. It's hard to understand that there are men who live for nothing, who have no goals, no ideas, no purpose. I had some suspicions about Tom Wernekink but the letter you brought from Rotterdam convinced me. Did you all read the letter?"

"Yes, sir," de Gier and Cardozo replied at the same time.

"A strange document. What did you think about it, de Gier?"

De Gier laughed. "I thought it was a good letter, sir."

"Why?"

De Gier was looking out the window.

"Why?" asked the commissaris again.

"A good letter," de Gier repeated.

"And you, Cardozo?"

"It irritated me a bit, sir. Man had a lot of chances, didn't he? Intelligent, a father with money, and yet he did nothing with his life. It was a suicide note in a way, an invitation to the Angel of Death. I believe life is worth living."

"He predicted his own death," the commissaris said slowly, "and probably very exactly. The details may have been right. A man in a dark suit with pointed shoes who killed him with a pistol shot. How could he have known?"

Grijpstra sat up. "That worried me too, sir, really worried me. I suspected that he might have known his killer but when I read the letter again I hesitated. What's your thought, sir?"

The commissaris waited a while before he answered.

"Just my thought," he said in the end. "Don't hold me to it. I think the man suffered, and suffered consciously. It may be possible to have very clear visions when you steer yourself into a situation like that. Most of us just live. We do what the current of our life steers us into. We think we make decisions but we don't really. Wernekink made a decision—he refused to conform and he kept on refusing. That letter proves it, I think, and also the way he lived. He refused to invite that girl into his house and she was throwing herself at him. He refused to be sensible."

"You think that's admirable?" Cardozo asked de Gier.

De Gier didn't reply.

"Don't be too sensible, Cardozo," the commissaris said softly. "If you do you'll never get further than the surface. In our work we have to go deeper sometimes. I think Wernekink was a very unusual man and I wouldn't be surprised if he had developed some unusual qualities."

De Gier was looking at Cardozo, smiling faintly.

||||| 14 /////

At eight-thirty that evening the commissaris' black Citroën parked at sixty-three Prince Alexander Street, right in front of a large dignified-looking mansion surrounded by a garden with larixes and pine trees. The car gracefully bobbed, first in front and then in the rear, as the tension of its suspension system hissed away in a long almost passionate sigh.

De Gier was irritated by the supercilious smile under the heavy mustache of the sleepy-eyed young constable at the wheel.

"You've done it again, hey?" de Gier asked.

"Yes, sergeant. When I need a parking space I find it."

It was true, of course. The commissaris' driver always did manage to find parking space close to or exactly where the commissaris wanted to go.

"Yes, yes," de Gier said. "I'm glad you didn't fall asleep

this time. I hear you nearly scraped off the side of the car some weeks ago. The police garage mechanics were telling me about it."

"An unfortunate accident," the constable said, "but not my fault. The other car should never have wigwagged in traffic. The other driver's insurance company will pay. I asked them yesterday. I'm in the clear."

"A responsible driver would have been able to avoid the smash," de Gier said. "It's a matter of refusing to take risks."

"Yes, de Gier," the commissaris said and put a hand on the sergeant's shoulder. The constable was looking straight ahead.

"Constable," the commissaris said, "I don't expect any problems but if we do run into trouble we'll blow a whistle. When you hear the whistle you can call for assistance on the radio. And don't go in by yourself; wait for a patrol car to arrive."

"Yes, do be careful," de Gier said and patted the constable on the shoulder. "And don't fall asleep," he hissed when the commissaris was opening the gate.

The constable wasn't in uniform that evening but he managed to look just as neat in a dark suit, white shirt and black tie.

"Have you got your pistol?" de Gier asked.

The constable patted his jacket. "Right here, sergeant."

"Don't use it," de Gier said, "whatever happens. You have an orange judo belt, haven't you?"

"Yes."

"You can practice some throws."

The constable took a deep breath as de Gier followed the commissaris through the gate.

"Lovely place," the commissaris said as they walked up the short driveway. Two white Mercedeses were parked under an enormous pine tree on the right. "A real old-fashioned villa. This house must date back to the time when this part of Amsterdam was still open country. The merchants built their summer homes here. It's seventeenth century, I think."

"It hasn't changed its purpose either," de Gier said. "The merchants of the Golden Age liked to have their parties where they wouldn't be disturbed. And this area is still quiet, far from the canals and the bustle of town. I don't think our friends will run into unexpected acquaintances in Prince Alexander Street. It's all homes for the elderly and private hospitals here. Nobody can afford to live in palaces like this now."

"Yes," the commissaris said. He was thinking of the note he had received from the tax collector that day. More to pay, always more to pay. The collector had never made a refund, not as far back as the commissaris could remember.

"Only Norway pays more tax than we do," he said to de Gier. "Did you know that?"

"I don't want to go to Norway," de Gier said. "I want to go to New Guinea. I had a post card from New Guinea yesterday. It was postmarked in Japen Island. It just said, "Greetings"; there was no signature."

The commissaris chuckled. "Was it addressed to Headquarters, de Gier?"

"Yes, sir; he doesn't remember my private address. He had been there once but has probably forgotten the number."

"Good luck to him," the commissaris said.

"This is as far as I go now," the commissaris said. "You ring the bell and show your card. I am going back to the car. Grijpstra's plan was all right. Tell the doorman to send his boss to the car and wait here."

De Gier rang the bell. It took some time before the door

opened. There was no name on the door. Nobody, not even
a suspicious and cynical policeman like de Gier, would
expect the mansion to be a brothel. He had time to look
around, to admire the magnificent oak doors, the fresh paint
on the window frames, the perfect layout of the garden.
There was even a pond and he saw the dim shapes of golden
carp flitting around among the large lily leaves.

"Sir?" a quiet voice asked.

He recognized the type immediately. A pimp, but a pimp
of the solid variety. A large, still handsome man in spite of
his years. The man would be close to sixty but his shoulders
hardly sagged. The sort of man who would never lose his
temper and who could pacify the screaming whore and the
obstreperous client and keep the whore's love and the client's
respect. There are all sorts of pimps. The flashy young
pimps never last long. They drink and get into fights and
a few years of the happy life turn them into crippled alco-
holics. There are also criminal pimps, who land up in jail.
But the quiet powerful pimp lasts. This was a quiet powerful
pimp.

De Gier had to look up when he spoke to the man. He
showed his card and the man took it from his hand and kept
it at arm's length.

"My eyes aren't what they used to be, sergeant." He was
speaking very softly.

"Get your boss," de Gier whispered back. "Tell him to
go outside. There is a black Citroën at the curb, and in it
your boss will find my boss. They are going to have a little
talk."

"Wait here, sergeant; I'll get him."

"No," de Gier said. "I am going with you."

The pimp smiled slowly. "Don't worry, sergeant. I'll
phone him. There's a phone in the hall."

The hall was vast, with a Persian carpet on the marble tiles and full-length statues of Greek nymphs, their stone robes falling down. The telephone stood on a brass Turkish table, next to an ornamental box cut out of mahogany.

"What's in the box," de Gier asked. He had noticed it was locked.

The pimp-doorman patted his stomach. "I have a key here that fits the lock. There are chips in the box. We don't believe in money blowing about the house. If you want anything I give you a chip."

"What do I give you?"

The doorman laughed. "Money, sergeant. You give me money and I give you chips. With chips you can amuse yourself in Villa Marshview. You can drink, you can take the ladies upstairs and you can gamble. And if you want a cigar I give it to you. Cigars are free."

"Give," de Gier said.

The doorman opened a drawer, hidden among the copper garlands of his table, and produced an enormous box of cigars. He opened it with a flourish. There were very thin delicate cigars in the box, and middle-sized cigars, and short fat cigars, and big cigars—big enough for the large toad-mouths of bankowners and shipbuilders.

"A big one," de Gier said. "One of those."

"But certainly, sir," the doorman said, and pulled at the thick golden chain that spanned his stomach. There was a key on the end of the chain, and a cigar cutter. He cut the cigar with a cruel twist and gave it to de Gier, who held the cigar between his teeth. The doorman reached into his waistcoat pocket and brought out a long match. He stood on one leg and scraped the match to life on the sole of his shoe.

"There you are, sir."

De Gier didn't thank him. He felt silly. The doorman had a strong personality and he could feel it ooze around him. He was glad he wasn't a woman. Women would collapse if this minor god deigned to bow down and pay attention to them.

"Boss," the doorman said. "Grand Alarm, boss. The police are here. They want you to come down immediately. In the hall. There's a car waiting for you."

He put the phone down and grinned. "That'll knock the shit out of him, sergeant. He scares easy, you know. He'll be falling down the stairs in a minute."

The doorman folded his hands on his back and watched the stairs. De Gier watched too. A small man just over five-feet tall and dressed in a striped suit, striped shirt and striped tie came running down. The stripes didn't match.

"What's this, Joop?" the man asked in a loud excited whisper. "Police? You aren't joking again are you?"

"No, boss. This is Sergeant de Gier, a detective. He showed me his card; it's a real card. And he wants you to go outside. There's a Citroën parked beyond the gate. Inside there's an officer who wants to talk to you."

"No," the boss whispered, "no, no. What's this? No trouble, surely! There's never any trouble here. A members' only club, sergeant, and you can't buy your membership at the door. We don't want any new members; we want it to be nice and cozy here. And the girls are all over twenty-one—married—most of them. No drugs. And the gambling is for laughs only. What's up, sergeant?"

De Gier made an inviting gesture toward the door.

"You saw the card, eh, Joop?" The doorman nodded, his face showed nothing, no matter how hard the boss stared. No help. No peaceful reassurance. "A police card, eh, Joop? We have no business with private detectives here."

"A police card, boss. Detective-sergeant the gentleman is. And the officer outside will be a chief inspector."

"Commissaris," de Gier said.

"Aw, shit!" The boss said. "A commissaris. What the hell does a commissaris want to see me for?"

"You have a bad conscience?" de Gier asked.

"No!" The boss stamped his foot. De Gier looked at the foot. It was protected by a shiny orange boot, fastened by two zips. The boot stamped again on the marble floor.

"Don't tap-dance," de Gier said. "It makes me nervous."

"No," the man almost shrieked. "I am telling you, nothing happens here that shouldn't happen. We never have complaints."

"The commissaris is waiting," de Gier said.

The boss rushed at the door.

"What's the trouble?" the doorman asked. "You can tell me, you know. I won't tap-dance. And he is right anyway. We never have complaints."

De Gier shrugged.

"A drink," the doorman suggested, "a nice long drink. Behind the bar is a black man from Jamaica who can mix drinks, long drinks. A tall glass with a bit of rum, some fruit juice and nice tinkling ice cubes. You can drink his concoctions all night and feel pleasant all the time. No headache in the morning. No sudden weakness if you happen to fall up the stairs. Here."

De Gier felt a chip in his hand. Green plastic, an inch square. It had the figure twenty-five printed into it, a silver twenty-five on a fond of pale green.

"Will buy you five hooplas," the doorman said, "and I'll give you another one when it runs out."

"Five guilders a drink?" de Gier asked.

"Drinks are cheap," the doorman explained, "and the

girls don't make you drink. You can buy them a drink if you really want to but they'll never ask for it. The bar will give them free lemonades or Cokes or sodas."

"And if you want the girls?"

"I don't want the girls," the doorman corrected. "You do. And if *you* do, you come to me and you buy a golden chip. A golden chip says one hundred. One hundred says a girl. And if you want the girl to cater to your special wishes you ask me for two golden chips. For two they'll satisfy your strangest desires, your craziest dreams. And if you can't find any because your subconscious is all clogged up by hard work and sad thoughts they'll suggest something. They'll act it for you and you'll never know that they're acting. Oh boy! Two chips will take you to heaven, and not to the part where harps are played on clouds. There are harps and clouds, of course, but that's for the ordinary. This place is for the extraordinary. This place is for *you*, sergeant."

The doorman had spoken softly and had bent down so that his face was level with de Gier's. It expressed an intense goodness. His deep voice reverberated in de Gier's resisting brain. The doorman's arms were spread out and his huge hands were open, about a foot away from de Gier's shoulders. De Gier felt the hands were protecting him, and vitalizing all his body juices at the same time.

De Gier stepped back and shook himself. "Stop that," he said. His voice was hoarse.

The doorman laughed. "Not bad, was it? It's my gimmick for the shy guest. Have done it a hundred thousand times but it still works. They say I should go on the stage but there's no money on the stage."

"There's plenty of money here!"

"Yes, sergeant," the doorman said. "There is. But what's

money? You guys always think we pimps work for money. But after a while money changes into paper. How many meals can I eat? How many cars can I drive? And how many suits can I wear?"

De Gier was looking at the doorman. He felt much better now that he had been released.

"No, I don't work for money anymore. Perhaps I never have."

"What do you work for?"

The doorman made a wide gesture, without pointing at anything in particular or indicating a certain direction. "Who knows? For this place perhaps. It's a great place and I enjoy being here. The boss owns most of it; he has brains— businessman's brains. But I own a bit of Villa Marshview myself, and it has a lot of my ideas. I don't know what's better, brains or ideas. And I like bringing in the women. We prefer them to be married, part-time, you know. They enjoy themselves more that way and the clients enjoy their enjoyment. They come here to earn themselves some pocket money, or a nice bright little motorcar, or a holiday, or a leather settee and matching chairs. We never try to hold them when they have had enough. There are always others."

"How do you get your women?"

"We advertise, or we used to advertise. Asked for host-esses. That's a good word: 'hostess.'" The doorman smacked his lips. "Makes them think they have class. Hostesses to the rich, to the famous. And they are, of course. We don't have poor clients. They come by themselves now. Some girlfriend tells them; they have tea together in a cozy place and natter away, and the next thing is that they come here. I open the door and there's a silly dumpy thing at the door, stuttering away. I bring her in and take her to a nice room. The Jamaican brings a little drink and we chat. Usually she is all right, just a little change here or there. Another dress, another way of walking, or perhaps she shouldn't wear a dress but velours jeans, or wide flowing trousers, or a gown, or something short and frilly. We don't want her to prance about naked."

"No striptease?" de Gier asked, sucking on his cigar.

"Sure. Must have a bit of striptease. They all strip. There's a little stage. On the stage they have to be sexy, show it all, loosen all the brakes. I encourage them; I train them even. I sit on a big chair and we go through the act, bit by bit. I get other girls to show them and if they happen to do something right I clap and shout and kiss them on the cheek, or pat their bottoms—depends on what sort of girl they are. But when the act is over they have to be demure again and wander around, talking and listening to the clients. Listening, that's very important."

"Information?" de Gier asked. "You want information."

"You're a proper policeman, aren't you?" the doorman asked. "No, no. We don't want information. What do you think we are? Blackmailers? We just want them to listen to the clients. Show interest, you know. The client is buying chips, isn't he? Lovely plastic chips. Go spend your chip, sergeant. There's your boss, and mine."

The commissaris was coming through the door that the boss was holding for him. The little man was still very nervous.

"Certainly, sir," he was saying. "Come right in, sir. I know what you want now. You really had me worried, you know. I am so glad I know what you want now."

"What does the commissaris want, boss?" the doorman asked.

"Ssh," the little man said. "Lock the door; we aren't

opening until nine-thirty anyway. Lock it and we'll go into my office. I'll explain it all to you."

"I think the sergeant wants a drink," the doorman said.

The commissaris looked at de Gier. "Do you want a drink, de Gier? What's that cigar?"

"No sir," de Gier said. "I don't want a drink. And the cigar is very nice; the doorman gave it to me."

The doorman offered the box to the commissaris, who selected the smallest cigar he could find. The doorman stood on one foot again and held a long match.

"Here we are," the little man said. "We'll go through the thing again. Make sure there is no mistake."

They were in a small office. It looked like any other office: a gray filing cabinet, a desk, gray low metal and plastic chairs for visitors, a typewriter, an electronic book-keeping machine. The little man was behind his desk, looking somewhat taller now, and the visitors were trying to find comfortable positions. The doorman leaned against the wall. He was too large to fit into the low chairs.

"It's about Mr. Sharif, Joop," the boss explained. "Mr. Sharif and his friends, or his staff I should say. You know them: four gentlemen who run his most important stores."

He was looking at the commissaris now. "They come here once a week, commissaris. We have a room upstairs where people can talk. A lot of business is done in that room. I don't know what goes on of course, but I have an idea sometimes. Just an idea, mind you. There are African gentlemen who want to equip armies—they buy tanks and airplanes—and there are businesses that want to join other businesses. The directors have a quiet chat here, feeling each other's propositions. Big deals. They talk, and we send up drinks. When they come down for the girls it's all fixed up. The deals, I mean. But I never know what goes on exactly. Joop and I provide the background, the entourage, the atmosphere."

"I see," the commissaris said. "And Mr. Sharif? What does he do here?"

The doorman laughed. "He fucks," he said.

"No, no, Joop," the boss said. "I wish you could forget that word. Sexual intercourse if you must describe it. Not that nasty word. Grow up, Joop."

"Puberty is in all of us," the doorman said.

"Yes, yes. Not in Mr. Sharif. I am surprised that he is in trouble, by the way. He has been coming here for years and years and I have never seen him lose his temper or heard him curse or even say a nasty word. He is a very dignified and cultured gentleman. And an important businessman. He meets his assistants here—once a week—but he has brought us other guests. I have seen the photographs of these other guests in the papers. No names, of course. I won't mention names. But Mr. Sharif's guests aren't nobodies."

"Right," the commissaris said. "He'll come at ten, won't he?"

"Yes, commissaris."

"And his assistants will arrive a little later, or a little earlier. Then they'll meet in your room. Do they stay long?"

"An hour at the most."

"I want to be able to hear them, and see them if possible. Can it be arranged?"

The boss was looking at the doorman.

"Yes," the doorman said. "My room is next to the conference room. I have a nice drill, bought it last week. I can drill two sets of holes."

"All right, so we can see. What about hearing them?"

"I don't like this," the boss said. "If Mr. Sharif finds out he won't be pleased."

"Leave Mr. Sharif to us," the commissaris said quietly. De Gier looked up, startled. There was a note of deadly venom in the commissaris', voice and the small body of the old man imperceptibly shuddered. De Gier, in the five years he had worked under the commissaris, had never seen this part of his character.

The doorman had looked up too. His quiet large eyes under their heavy brows studied the little figure in the corner of the office.

"You can handle Mr. Sharif, commissaris?" the doorman asked.

"Yes," the commissaris said, very softly, but the word penetrated into every corner of the room.

"A microphone," the boss said. "You're clever with electric things. Can you help out, Joop?"

"The combo has a spare microphone downstairs," the doorman said. "And there's plenty of flex, but we don't want to show any of it. I'll see what I can do. Do you want a tape recorder connected to it?"

"Yes," de Gier said. "We'll have a look at the room together. I can help you, I think, and I have a good tape recorder in the car."

"You two had better start," the commissaris said.

The boss jumped up from behind his desk. "We can go to the bar, commissaris. It's more comfortable down there."

"Don't call me 'commissaris.'"

"No, sir, sorry, sir. I'll call you 'sir.'"

"That'll be better."

"What about Mr. Sharif and his men, sir? You won't arrest them on the premises, will you?"

"No," the commissaris said, "not if we can help it. They

don't know the sergeant and they don't know me. We just want to listen in for a while. Afterward we can watch them in the bar, while they're enjoying themselves."

The boss tried to laugh. "Yes. I'll give you some chips. Money is never spent in the house. Joop will give you as many chips as you like."

"We'll buy the chips," the commissaris said.

"Very well, sir. So there will be no trouble for the house, will there, sir?"

"Do as you're told," the commissaris said.

"Yes, sir."

⫶⫶⫶⫶ 15 ⫶⫶⫶⫶

"Gentlemen," Sharif said, "I welcome you."

There was a murmur from the table. Four men, dressed in suits, white shirts and ties, were watching him with attention. They looked neat enough but their appearance contrasted sharply with the elegant figure at the head of the table. The Arab was wearing a light suit, impeccably tailored. His handsome face with the aquiline nose and slightly slanting dark brown eyes was calm. His black hair, which he wore fairly long, shone with a natural gloss. His long brown hands were on the table, lying absolutely still as if they weren't part of him. He looked at the four men one by one.

"Allow me to come to the point immediately. We come here for business and pleasure, and we don't want to make the pleasure wait too long."

The four men smiled.

Sharif smiled too, but there was no eagerness in his face. "Well then. There has been a disturbance. An unfortunate disturbance. Our most important supplier of reasonably prices goods is out of business. For good, I am afraid. His organization is shattered, which is a pity. It was an organization that worked and that I had hoped to fuse into ours, making one of you its director. We were making some headway and now this."

He paused. "I have picked you personally, each one of you. You have worked for our business for a number of years. Each one of you has a history that has qualified him for his place in our organization. You have brains; you are cool. You must stay cool."

Sharif inclined his head. "You, my friend, are a fighting man. You fought in the Far East; you're a brave man, a warrior. And you, my friend, have crossed a sea in a small boat, a great adventure, which you brought to a successful ending. And you, my friend, spent many years in my country. You speak my language. We can read each other's thoughts. And you, my friend, have connections that you have never misused and who have never failed us. We must combine our talents and weather this little storm. Each one of you runs one of our main stores. The police detectives have visited your stores. Did they find any traces of moved merchandise?"

Two men said, "No." Two hesitated.

"What happened?" Sharif asked.

The man he was looking at lit a cigarette.

"They didn't say anything, Sharif, but they may have seen something. I didn't like the way they left. Perhaps they spoke to one of the employees who helped me shift the merchandise. I had to work quickly and I couldn't get it all into the truck by myself."

"And you. What happened in your store?"

"There was some confusion in my store, Sharif," the man said slowly. "A wrong TV set stayed behind; a right one was moved out. The detectives took the numbers of all the sets in the store. If they check your books in the head office they may stumble into an irregularity."

"I see," Sharif said, and folded his hands. "I see; I am glad you're telling me. Mistakes will be made. It's a condition we humans must always take into account. There are detectives going through our books now, comparing invoices with lists of numbers. The TV sets and the other merchandise came from containers that our supplier secured. There must be lists of the numbers of missing TV sets. Yes. It's bad. But perhaps it will not be noticed. Did anything else go wrong?"

He looked at his men one by one. Nobody said anything.

"The Cat," one of the men said.

"He is in jail. I believe he won't stay there. His connection with us was never proved. The Cat is a wily animal, proud and free. He will be sleeping on his bunk, smiling at the policemen who try to talk to him."

"Half his mustache is gone."

"Yes," Sharif said, "so I heard. He will look slightly ridiculous but in Amsterdam half a mustache is not as strange as it would be in other places." Sharif laughed, a gentle deep-throated laugh.

"Someone died on the dike, I heard," one of the men said.

"That was planned," another man said and chuckled. "The Flyer did well. There's no trace, only a bullet."

Sharif raised a hand. "This is a meeting, gentlemen, a business meeting. We must abide by our rules. Let me direct the meeting and let no one talk out of place."

Sharif was looking at the ceiling. When his eyes came down the four men were staring straight ahead. "There has been death on the dike," Sharif said. "Unplanned stupid death. A man was shot in the stomach by the police and he is now dead in hospital. Another man has died but the shot was directed and fired quietly; it came from the dark of night and a jinni slipped away and was never seen again. The jinni has no name. If the jinni is named, a person is created and a person has habits, leaves tracks, lives in a house. The police can put a hand on his shoulder. We must allow the jinni to be."

"So what now?" a man asked.

"We wait," Sharif said. "The Cat will be free one day but we must not talk to him again. We will play the Cat's game ourselves now and our warrior will train some men to master the tricks that are necessary. The men will be reliable. There will be some Arabs and there will be some local men. And a woman perhaps—a good woman—who we will find in the house we are in now. But first we wait. We may have to wait six months or a year, but we can afford to wait. Gentlemen?" Sharif asked.

He looked at them one by one for agreement. "Excellent. We will end the meeting. I will see you downstairs in a minute. I thank you for your presence."

The men stood as Sharif left the room.

He looked regal.

A sheik sweeping out of his tent, de Gier thought. There'll be a white racing camel outside and he'll be far away soon, swallowed by the desert.

⫸ 16 ⫷

THE DOORMAN LED DE GIER BACK TO THE CAR WHERE HE handled the tape recorder to the constable at the wheel. Neither the doorman, nor de Gier, nor the sleepy-eyed constable saw the small dark man who had been standing in the garden opposite for some time now. The man stood next to the heavy trunk of a larix, his body hidden by the tree's low branches.

De Gier and the doorman went back into the house. The commissaris was at the bar, sipping from a drink that the smiling fat bartender had prepared in a most professional manner. He handled the silver shaker as if he were welcoming a royal personage who had the right to an extravagant show of pure joy. A young lady was sitting next to the commissaris. De Gier stopped to admire her. She was dressed in a long black gown, buttoned up to her small chin and enclosing a long slender neck. Her face was innocence itself and the little red mouth pouted. Her leg on the commissaris' side was bare and she moved it every few seconds. The naked thigh made de Gier gasp. The slit in the gown closed as de Gier joined the commissaris.

"Evening, sir," de Gier said. "I didn't expect you to be here tonight. I thought you were still in France."

"Hello, Rinus," the commissaris said, smiling delightedly. "I was hoping to meet you here. How are things at the office? Meet our charming hostess. Her name is Charlotte. Charlotte meet Rinus, my right hand in the firm. You two are very well suited, I think."

The girl jumped down from her stool and bowed low. Then she lifted her face and offered her mouth. De Gier kissed her lightly while the commissaris tittered.

"Excellent," he said. "You two *are* suited, I see. I was right."

"Of course," the girl said.

"Can I buy you a drink, Charlotte," de Gier asked.

"No, thanks. I still have some in my glass, but we can dance if you like. Let me introduce you both to Ella. We can't leave our friend at the bar by himself, can we."

"Who is Ella?" the commissaris asked.

Charlotte pointed to a redheaded girl sitting by herself at the other side of the bar.

"She is beautiful," the commissaris said, "but I would prefer that lovely Chinese girl who just came in. If you don't mind, of course. It's no reflection on your taste at all; it's just that I am charmed by the wisdom of the Far East."

"You are a dear," Charlotte said and brushed her hair past the commissaris' cheek. "Just a minute, please."

"Everything all right?" the commissaris asked.

"Yes, sir. The recorder is back in the car and the doorman has cleaned up the conference room."

"This is Thsien-niu," Charlotte said. "Did I pronounce your name right, Thsien-niu?"

The girl smiled and bowed, a tiny bow that didn't do much more than acknowledge the presence of the two men.

Tricks, de Gier thought. Tricks that they learn from the podgy pimp. He saw Joop, the doorman, in the classroom upstairs, his huge body slumped on a couch while the girls performed. He inspired them with his warm deep voice that slurred and caressed its words and he made the girls glow with pleasure, obedience and humility.

"Sit next to me, Thsien-niu," the commissaris said, trying to pronounce the foreign sounds properly.

"Please," the girl said in English while she jumped lightly onto the high stool.

"Thsien-niu doesn't speak Dutch yet," Charlotte said, "but she is learning quickly and her English is wonderful. She comes from Hong Kong. She is very popular here."

De Gier was on the small dance floor with Charlotte's gowned body pressed against him. The combo, consisting of three young men—all dressed in dark suits with narrow trousers and white fluffy open-necked shirts with dark blue scarves—played a slow shuffle, very easy to get into. They often stopped, letting four bars go by. The pianist's right hand played a simple combination of high notes with a loose touch. The left hand, drums and double bass came in together, stressing the combination and making it run up de Gier's spine. He had his hands on the girl's shoulders and pulled her against his chest but she wriggled free and began a dance on her own, four feet away from him. She stuck to the same place, hardly moving her feet but making her body shiver and de Gier, led by the piano's high notes, improvised a merry-go-round without overdoing it. He was using a proper pattern for his feet, which he remembered from dance lessons twenty years ago. But he had never been taught by the old lady of the school to use his shoulders, his arms and his hands. It had been kind of the old lady not to teach him, for now he could do as he liked and he was doing well. The commissaris approved, studying him from the bar, and the Chinese girl smiled vaguely as she saw the tall athletic man change into a little boy and then gradually begin to find his own strength again. De Gier had no thoughts while he danced; he was aware of a feeling of well-being. He had become part of the music.

"Beautiful man," the Chinese girl said to the commissaris.

"Yes," the commissaris said. "Don't tell him; it makes him feel silly."

"That's good," the girl said. "You want to dance too?"

"No. Let's drink."

The barman came before he was called. The crushed ice in his silver flask moved with the rhythm of the shuffle and the commissaris' and the girl's glasses were filled.

Sharif came into the bar, followed by his four men, who were grinning with pleasure in anticipation. There were more girls in the bar now and some twelve men. Other couples had joined de Gier and Charlotte on the dance floor and the combo, feeling that the shuffle had caught on, allowed some exuberance to glide into the music. The pianist's right hand was now rather complicated and the double bass had a chance to exert itself; it was good enough to play by itself and the pianist sat back, smiling at the drummer, who only stressed the vibrations of the giant violin by softly hitting a cymbal.

Sharif separated from his companions and came to the bar. The commissaris smiled at him and Sharif stopped.

"Virgins as fair as corals and rubies," Sharif said. "Which of your Lord's blessings would you deny?"

"This is hardly the place I would come to deny myself anything," the commissaris said. "Can I offer you a drink?"

"You can," Sharif said, "but there should not be alcohol in it. And there's nothing right now I can offer in return, except perhaps my company."

The barman, who had seen Sharif join the commissaris from the other end of the bar, was hovering around them already and poured a glass of an almost black liquid.

"The juice of blackberries," Sharif said, raising the glass. "A rare delicacy but I have noticed nobody here likes it. I always find the contents of the bottle at the same level as I left it on my last visit. Yet it mixes with alcohol, I think, although I have never tried it."

"You don't drink at all?" the commissaris asked.

"Never. I am an Arab."

"Which of your Lord's blessings would you deny?" the commissaris asked.

"Ah," said Sharif, "you remembered. A sentence from the Koran: Noah, one of its first chapters. Perhaps you think I was blaspheming?"

There was no glimmer of amusement in Sharif's large dark eyes as he scrutinized the commissaris' face.

"No," the commissaris said. "To blaspheme is to be childish and you do not strike me as a childish man. But to be able to drink is a blessing and you have asked me whether I would deny it?"

"I was referring to other pleasures," Sharif said. "And I do not agree with you that alcohol is a blessing. When I was younger and sillier I tasted alcohol. And I have been very drunk. It took weeks to forget the imbecilities I uttered during those few hours. I woke up in a large building where streetcars are parked during the night. I was lying with my head on a rail. I could never remember how I got into that building but waking up was waking up in hell, and even now I have a fear of streetcars, especially at night. I have never drunk again."

"I see," the commissaris said. "Please meet my companion; her name is Thsien-niu."

"We are acquainted. How are you this evening, vision from heaven?"

The girl smiled.

"You are in business?" Sharif asked, sipping his blackberry juice.

The commissaris laughed and immediately excused himself. "When I was a child," the commissaris said, "I suffered from constipation. My mother would prepare porridge for me, a porridge of gray cement with lumps moving about in it. To give it flavor, and to mask the taste of the olive oil that she poured into it when she thought I wasn't looking, she would add half a glass of blackberry juice."

"Haha," Sharif said and there was real amusement on his face now. His eyes were slanting more than usual and there was a glitter of gold between his lips. "Perhaps the juice is to you what the streetcars in the evening are to me. Every man has his fears. Are you in business?"

"Construction," the commissaris said, "and you?"

"Secondhand clothes," Sharif said. "A small but profitable line, and a trade reserved for my race. The Jews are my competitors but we are all of the same family although they deny the truth. It's a pity. Acceptance of the truth would lead to harmony, harmony would lead to prosperity, prosperity would make more people discard their clothes quicker and my business would grow."

The commissaris leaned back against the bar and extended an arm. Thsien-niu snuggled into the arm and the commissaris' right hand rested lightly on her shoulder. She had an unlit cigarette in her mouth and as Sharif's hand shot out, his heavy golden lighter spat a small flame.

"Construction is big business," Sharif said modestly. "I imagine your company is responsible for the growth of this city and the large buildings that are rising in the south and that I admire from my window sometimes."

"Construction is a big business," the commissaris agreed, "but not always profitable. It makes for being busy and running about and..."

"And talk," Sharif said. "Much talk. Here at the bar. They talk to one another and they drop their voices but the catchwords sound up. Mumble, mumble, mumble—one million guilders—mumble, mumble, mumble, mumble—one hundred thousand guilders."

"There is no money in the secondhand clothes trade?" the commissaris asked.

Sharif laughed and made a gesture so that the barman unscrewed the top of his silver flask and the commissaris' glass filled up again.

"No," Sharif said. "Secondhand clothes are best kept in quietness."

De Gier came back from the dance floor.

"Where's Charlotte?" the commissaris asked.

"She is going to take her clothes off," de Gier said and looked at Sharif. "She'll be on stage soon."

"Mehemed el Sharif," Sharif said.

"Schol," de Gier said. "Rinus Schol; glad to meet you, sir."

"A schol," Sharif said slowly. "A fish, I believe. A flat fish that swims about and suddenly, quicker than it knows the reason why, flaps its tail, dives and ducks into the sand. The pursuer goes on and never sees."

"My assistant," the commissaris said. "My right hand in the office. Schol has learned more about the construction business in ten years than I have learned in thirty."

"The modest guide the clever," Sharif said.

"Excuse me, sir," the doorman said. "I have a call for you; will you take it in the hall?"

Sharif moved to the hall.

"Trouble," the doorman said to the commissaris. "Watch it."

The commissaris looked up. "How?"

"First door to the left. Turn right, go through the corridor and out through the garden door. Run to the car. You have a man in your car. Maybe he knows what's going on. Sharif is talking to another Arab in the hall now, his driver. You talk to your driver."

De Gier ran through the garden and swung himself over the stone wall. He dived into the back of the black Citroën.

"What did you see?" he asked the constable.

"That was quick," the driver said. "I hardly recognized you when you jumped the wall. I thought you were a bat."

"I was a fish just now," de Gier said. "What did you see?"

"After you left—you and that doorman—and had given me the tape recorder," the constable said, "I saw a man move in the garden opposite. A small man. He must have been there for some time."

"He is the Arab's driver—the Arab we are after," de Gier said. "He has a white Lincoln, which must be parked close by."

"Didn't see it. But the driver must have seen you putting the recorder in the car. He waited and I pretended to be asleep in the car. Now he is in the house."

"I am going back," de Gier said.

"Will you be long?"

"Perhaps. There is a beautiful girl in there taking her clothes off. On a stage. I am going to smoke a cigar while I watch her. A big cigar."

"Pfah!" the constable said.

"You go back to sleep. Maybe you'll see another Arab."

De Gier flitted back, as quickly as he had come. He was back at the bar when Sharif returned.

Charlotte had unzipped her gown and a trumpet player had joined the combo. He wailed as the zip came down, shrieked as the whiteness of her breasts shimmered in the pale light of the stage, and pulsated as the gown dropped to the floor. Charlotte danced and the muted trumpet became sad. The combo went back into its shuffle and the lights went out and on. The stage was empty. The dance had been the same dance that she had shared with de Gier twenty minutes before, but now she had been alone, alone with all the men in the bar.

"Very good," Sharif said and clapped. "She is like a woman I saw in Port Said, long ago. I wasn't supposed to watch her since I worked in the kitchen, but I always sneaked out when she was on stage."

"Where's Schol?"

"There," the commissaris said and grinned. There were three leather chairs facing the small stage. De Gier was in the middle chair, smoking the butt of a large cigar that the doorman had given him. He was still looking at the stage.

"Your assistant knows how to enjoy himself. He is sincere. The other men pretended they were not really watching. Those chairs are always empty. Why have I never seen you before?"

"I have been here before," the commissaris said, "but we must have missed each other."

"Possibly," Sharif said.

"They suspect something," de Gier said as he stood next to the commissaris in the lavatory. "Sharif's driver saw me take the tape recorder to the car. He may not have seen that it was a tape recorder since it is dark outside and he was watching us from the other side of the street. I had it under my jacket but he must have seen that I gave something to the constable. And he reported on it."

"Yes," the commissaris said. "We'd better go. Or, rather, I will go. It's a pity they suspect us but it can't be helped. We may as well use the situation. Stay here and I'll send two detectives. They'll have to arrest the weakest of Sharif's helpers. I was watching them at the bar. One of them wears a striped tie, dark blue and white. I think he is worried. He's drinking a lot and he talks all the time—cracks jokes and laughs before the others laugh. He is the one who said that one of the wrong TV sets was left in his store. The detectives can play on that. I don't think he'll crack but the fact that he is arrested will shake Sharif. I'll tell them to sit at the bar until you give them a sign. Point at the man with your cigar when Sharif isn't watching."

"And then, sir?"

"Catch a cab and come to Headquarters. I'll see what I can find out about this Flyer they were talking about. The shadow who killed Tom Wernekink. We'll have to find him quickly, tonight if possible. I'll also get Grijpstra and Cardozo."

Someone came into the lavatory. The commissaris went

to the washstand and made a fuss with the tap, screwing it into exactly the right position so that the hot water would make his hands foam. He dried his hands briskly.

Sharif was still at the bar and the commissaris sat down next to him. The redhaired girl was on the stage now but Sharif was talking to Thsien-niu, who immediately moved away when she saw the commissaris and snuggled into his arm again.

"The lady from the Far East likes you," Sharif said. "It shows good taste."

"Do you like me?" the commissaris asked.

"Yes," Thsien-niu said. "I would like to go upstairs with you."

Sharif smiled. "An invitation hard to refuse."

"I am an old man," the commissaris said.

"I will sing for you."

"In Chinese?" Sharif asked. He was leaning forward.

"I can only sing in Chinese," the girl said, "and all the songs I know are about the sea. My father used to say that he could hear the sea when I sang to him. My country consists of islands; the sea is close."

"Sometimes," Sharif said, "I am glad I am no longer a young man. The mind of a young man is like the porno magazines that stare at you from every sixth shop window nowadays. A young man's thoughts, when he is with a woman he hasn't made yet, make him see images of shrimps wriggling in a glass full of mayonnaise. He is so filled with the urge to make the human race continue that he can think of nothing but the desire to fill the hole, the moist mysterious hole that will suck him up and hold him. For a while. But the girl talks about singing and he doesn't hear. Now that I am old I can hear." Sharif drank a little more of his blackberry juice.

* * *

"Give," de Gier said to the doorman.

The doorman held the cigar box and de Gier grabbed.

"Don't grab," the doorman said.

"Stand on one foot again," de Gier said.

The doorman stood on one foot and lit a match.

"Thanks. Soon two detectives will come and arrest one of your clients. Not Sharif, but one of his friends. They'll be very polite and take him away."

"The boss won't like it," the doorman said.

"No. But it can't be helped. You better see to it that the combo is going and that there's a girl on the stage when they make the arrest."

"You aren't going to make a fuss about this place afterward, are you, sergeant?" the doorman said. "We've been in business for a long time and we're used to it. I wouldn't know what to do with myself if this place is closed down. I am too old to start another one."

"No," de Gier said, "at least not if I can help it. You have some sort of license, don't you?"

"We are a club; we have a license for liquor and dancing and all that..."

"All that...?"

The doorman had his hands on his back and was slowly moving backward and forward.

"Yes, yes, you have a point," the doorman said. De Gier began to move toward the bar.

"Wait," the doorman said. "Perhaps you would like to be a member. Come here once in a while. Get a few chips. Sit in the leather chair near the stage and watch the show. You were very decorative in there. The girls like a man to watch them with some concentration."

"No," de Gier said.

* * *

"No, dear," the commissaris said. "Perhaps some other time but tonight I go home early. I am expecting some foreign visitors tomorrow and I'll have to be awake when they march into my office. But thank you for the invitation; I appreciate it."

"You are welcome," Thsien-niu said.

"A pity," Sharif said. "I enjoyed your company. Especially the story about the porridge you ate when you were a child."

De Gier came in from the hall, the cigar between his teeth. Thsien-niu giggled.

"That cigar is too big for you, Rinus," the commissaris said.

"It has a very nice taste, sir," de Gier said and took the cigar out of his mouth.

"Talk to Mr. Sharif and Thsien-niu," the commissaris said. "I have to go home. See you tomorrow."

"Sir," de Gier said.

The detectives came in twenty minutes later. The combo went into a session with the trumpet. The pianist's body was rigid, his head bent right down to the keyboard. The drums and the trumpet were in an orgy of sound and the bass thumped away while a tall slim Negress was back in the native jungle of her forefathers, moving around the stage in a trance of rhythmical lust. As de Gier's cigar pointed to the man with the striped tie, the detectives standing next to the man touched his arm and showed their police cards. Sharif's eyes followed the three men walking toward the hall.

Outside an unmarked police car had found the white Lincoln. Sharif came out of the house and walked down the driveway. The young Arab opened the door. The white car turned a corner and the police car followed.

De Gier telephoned for a cab.

Within twenty minutes he reported at Headquarters. Grijpstra was telephoning and Cardozo listening in.

"Where's the commissaris?" de Gier asked.

"He'll be right back. He is in the cell block talking to the Cat. Grijpstra is talking to the computer people; they're trying the computer's memory with the word 'Flyer.'"

"That's all we know," de Gier said.

"It may be enough," Cardozo said. "There can't be too many Flyers about."

"Thanks," Grijpstra said, "I'll wait. Phone Headquarters and ask for Adjutant Grijpstra. Don't be too long."

Grijpstra turned round. "There you are. You were in a brothel." His voice was full of reproach.

"Yes," de Gier said. "It was very nice. There was a naked Negress on the stage when I left and before her there were other women. I danced with one of them. She danced very well. And I have smoked two Cuban cigars and I have had a few drinks. And the music! Oh, Grijpstra, you should have heard the music."

"What music?"

"Trumpet. And the piano! Blues, a blues that never stopped. Not too slow. But exact. None of this playing about. It all fitted. The place is a villa called Marshview and it's run by a six-and-a-half-foot doorman. He oozes charm and he has trained the girls. Class. Real class."

"Did you play your flute?"

"No."

"Why not?"

"I was in the construction business. The commissaris

too. Building. The commissaris had just come back from France and I was his right hand. We met by accident. Worked for the same company. He was one of the big bosses."

"And you?"

"An executive. Promising material."

"It wasn't like that, was it?" Cardozo asked.

"Like what?"

"Like you said. I have been to brothels too. Horrible. They make you drink sweet champagne and the curtains are red velvet. There are mirrors and the women hang about on settees and the place stinks of perfume."

"Yes," Grijpstra said, "and the women call you 'sweetie' and 'duckie' and they talk to each other—right over your head—and they show porno films in a little room that smells of piss."

"No, no," de Gier said. "Like I said. A good place. Ask the commissaris."

"Bull," Cardozo said.

"Class," de Gier said stubbornly. "You should have seen that Negress dance. You could feel the jungle behind her. The moon. Palm trees. Drums throbbing. The round huts of the village behind you, and the warriors standing in a half circle, jingling the shells on their feet. Short sounds, you know. And when they jingle their shells the woman moves. Slowly. And her breasts are glistening and her hips shake a little—just a little. Her arms are stretched out and the moon is rising, a full white disc filling the sky."

"You saw all that?" Cardozo asked.

"It was there," de Gier said.

\\\\\\\\ 17 /////

"My lawyer seemed pretty sure that you would have to let me go today," the Cat said. He was sitting on his bunk and the commissaris was sitting opposite him on a low stool.

"There isn't much to do in these cells," the Cat said. "Did you have a look at that stool before you sat down?"

The commissaris got up and looked at the stool.

"It looks worn," the commissaris said.

"Worn!" The Cat got up and stretched. His hands touched the ceiling. "Wooden stools don't wear. That little bit of furniture was scratched, scratched by human hands. I have been studying it. It's worth a fortune I tell you. It can be put up for display in the Municipal Museum and it'll draw crowds. It's a perfect work of art. A wooden surface scratched by ten thousand human nails, patiently, eight hours a day. It's a work of harmony as well."

"Yes," the commissaris said. "Very interesting. But to appreciate it properly I would have to spend some time in this cell."

The Cat crossed his arms on his chest and bowed. "Be my guest, commissaris."

"It's an experience that isn't altogether new to me," the commissaris said.

"You have been in jail?"

"A little more than a year."

"How did you manage that?"

"A riddle for you to solve," the commissaris said. "You'll have something to do tomorrow."

The Cat frowned. "I've got it. The war! You were in the Resistance. You're the right age."

"Right."

"You'll have to give me a better riddle, commissaris."

"Why are we here?" the commissaris asked.

"Here in jail, you mean? Why are we here together, just now? In this cell?"

The commissaris smiled. The Cat smiled too. The commissaris looked very neat. He was sitting on the stool as if it had been specially made for him. His thin legs were neatly parallel, and the creases in his trousers were like two lines out of a geometrical drawing. The buttoned waistcoat, the thin chain of his watch, the narrow tie with its small knot, the wizened face with the two bright inquisitive but gentle eyes and the thin carefully combed hair, were all details that added up to an image inspiring confidence. A loving father, a teacher, an uncle, a friend of the family.

"No," the commissaris said. "The second riddle is more difficult."

"You mean why we are here, you and I, on Earth?"

The commissaris smiled.

"Do you read science fiction, commissaris?"

"I do sometimes."

"Yes," the Cat said. "It was only when I began to read science fiction that I understood something about the riddle. I didn't solve it, of course, but I knew then that there *is* a riddle. What the hell is all this life doing on a little round ball, suspended in space? You and me, and the guards who feed me, and Tom Wernekink and those fools on the dike."

"And Sharif," the commissaris said.

"And Sharif."

"Listen here," the commissaris said. "Sit down on your bunk and listen. You have to help me. I've got to get Wernekink's killer."

The Cat took the pillow off his bunk, punched it into shape and sat down, propping it behind his back.

"Yes, commissaris. I abhor violence. Tom Wernekink wanted to die, as you probably know, but I don't think a man should have crept into his garden to hide and wait and fire a pistol. No, he shouldn't have."

"You are a suspect, Cat, and anything you say can be used against you. Still I want you to tell me what you know."

The Cat laughed and his gaiety filled the small cell.

"You have to say that now, don't you?"

"It's the new law."

"Not a bad law. The suckers should be warned. It's their good right. But I won't tell you anything I shouldn't tell you at this stage. So far you have little against me, except this idiotic half mustache, which you won't let me shave off, and the fact that your detectives caught me while I was running about in my own garden."

"We have more now," the commissaris said. "That's why I could keep you in this cell for another two days. We checked the shops Sharif owns and found some nervous people there. They had been shifting the stolen merchandise but one of them slipped up and there's a TV set on Sharif's premises that came from your people on the dike. We are checking the lists now and the registration number of the TV will tally eventually. We have arrested the shop manager, who is being interrogated right now. He'll crack and tell us where we'll find the rest of the merchandise. And nine of your people are in the cells as well. A lot of fingers are pointing at you, Cat, and together they'll make the hand that will grab you. You'll be convicted of receiving. It's your first offense, so you won't be in jail long, but we'll win the case."

"You will," the Cat said, "but you haven't won yet and why should I make it easy?"

"No reason. Play the game as well as you can and we'll play ours. But the killer is a different game; we're on the same side. What do you know about the Flyer?"

"The Flyer," the Cat said. "You have a name. That's something."

"It's the name of a shadow. We need a real name."

"All right," the Cat said. "It seems to me now that I had a vision one night while half-asleep in Ursula's arms. It was after a dinner of snails and toast with some olives on the side. You want to hear about the vision?"

"Yes, please."

"It seems," the Cat said sleepily, "that a certain man with a feline name—a man who looks like me perhaps—was annoyed by a certain Arabic gentleman. He was doing business with the Arab and the Arab wanted more and more. So the man began to study the Arab and he sent out some spies, some little mice who ran about the Arab. And the mice heard that the Arab owned a dangerous tool—a human tool—a walking automatic pistol, that never misses. It was a strange tool, for it could also fly, on silent wings, like a moth."

"You mean it could glide," the commissaris said.

"Yes, glide."

"A glider," the commissaris said. "And where does this tool have his wings?"

"In Middelburg," the Cat said.

"The apparition has no name?"

"It will have a name, but I don't know it. It will eat three times a day and live in a house. It will also be sick, since a tool that kills for a price can't be put together properly. It will be dangerous."

"When you had this vision that night after the meal of snails and olives," the commissaris said, "didn't it occur to you that you might try to catch this deadly moth?"

"No, sir," the Cat said. "I believe in cleverness, not in violence. Violence flies in a small circle and burns its own wings."

"So does cleverness, perhaps," the commissaris said. "Is the vision completely described?"

"I saw no more."

The commissaris got up. "Is there anything I can do for you, Cat?"

"I have three wishes," the Cat said and got up too.

"Go ahead."

"First, I would like you to leave your tin of cigars behind with a box of matches."

The commissaris patted his pocket, produced the tin of cigars and the matches and put them on the Cat's bunk.

"Second, I would like to have the thick dark blue book that is on the floor next to my bed at home."

"I'll ask one of my men to pick it up tomorrow and deliver it to you."

"Thank you. And third, I would like you to send a telegram to Ursula's father in Australia. She is mentally disturbed. She has been treated for a while and is functioning again but with me locked up she'll be alone and may get into all sorts of psychic trouble. I want her father to fly out here and pick her up. She should be at home with her family. Her father is rich and he loves her. He'll come when you wire him. I'll give you the address if you lend me your pen."

The commissaris took out his pen. "All right, I'll send the wire straightaway."

"Thank you. Good hunting."

The commissaris knocked on the cell door; they heard the shuffling footsteps of the guard in the narrow corridor outside.

"We've got something, sir," Grijpstra said when the commissaris returned to his office.

"Tell me."

"The computer knows the Flyer. A hired gun who was employed at the beginning of last year in the case of the illegal distillers in the south. The police found out about the distilleries because one of the owners turned up dead in the forest, with a bullet between his eyes. The killer was never named but his nickname was: the Flyer. The theory was that one distiller tried to buy out another and the man refused, so he got shot. But nothing was proved; there are some men in jail now, but they were only charged with manufacturing spirits without a license. I have the name of the chief inspector who dealt with the case but he is retired now and lives in France. There is no telephone number. The files will be available in the morning. I telephoned the record office but the only man who knows his way about there isn't on duty and isn't at home either. They are short staffed, it seems. We'll have to wait till tomorrow."

"No," the commissaris said, "the Flyer is a glider pilot who lives in Middelburg. I want to go there now. What about Sharif? Did the car following him report?"

"Yes, sir," de Gier said, "Sharif went home. The police car left but there's another one there now—a car from our shadow department—with a sergeant and a female constable in it. If Sharif leaves again they'll follow him and report back to Headquarters if anything happens."

The commissaris grinned. "Right. That's very nice. How did you get the shadow car?"

"I spoke to their chief, sir. He had a car in town that had nothing special to do. It's a very nice car too, a new Porsche."

The telephone buzzed and de Gier picked it up. "Radio room," the voice said. "We've had a report from the Porsche. Your suspect left his house in a gray Jaguar and is now leaving the city, direction south; the Porsche is after him. Your suspect is accompanied by another man, a small dark-skinned man who is driving. Do you want me to give a message to the Porsche?"

"Yes," de Gier said. "Tell them to keep on reporting and to pass the messages to Detective-Constable Cardozo, who will be in this office."

"De Gier," the commissaris said.

"Sir."

"Tell them not to interfere with Sharif. Just follow and report."

De Gier passed the message and put the phone down.

"Stay here, Cardozo," the commissaris said. "We'll phone you. The radio in the car can't cover a lot of distance. The Porsche will also be phoning. You'll have to be the center of communication tonight."

"Yes, sir."

"Get the car, de Gier; it's parked in the courtyard. My driver will go with us. If he gets too sleepy you or Grijpstra can take over for him. We are going to Middelburg."

"Sir," de Gier said.

⫶⫶⫶ 18 ⫻⫻

"Good evening," the commissaris said to the desk sergeant at Middelburg's small police station. "We are from the Amsterdam Municipal Police." He showed his card.

"Commissaris," the desk sergeant said in an awed voice. "Please come in, sir. Can I get you some coffee? There's a fresh pot. I always make one at four o'clock in the morning; keeps me awake. There'll be enough for three cups."

"Thank you, sergeant. Can you find us an officer? We have some work to do here and it would be nice if we could do it immediately."

"I'll phone the inspector on standby duty."

"Please."

The commissaris took the other phone and dialed the telegraph office. He dictated the cable to Ursula's father, spelling each word, and told the girl to charge the cost to the Amsterdam police. Then he phoned his own office.

"Any news, Cardozo?"

"Yes, sir; where are you, sir?"

"Middelburg police station."

"Good. Sharif should be close to you. The Porsche followed him to the Zeeland bridge but lost him just after the bridge. They are in Goes now, waiting near a phone. They want further instructions."

"Tell them to go home and thank them. Do you have the number of that Jaguar?"

"Yes, sir. I'll give it to you, and please give me your telephone number over there."

"Stay near that phone, Cardozo," the commissaris said before he hung up. "It'll be boring but we may need you again, although it's unlikely. You can go to sleep if you like as long as you are close to the phone."

"Yes, sir. I'll be here."

"Poor Cardozo," de Gier said.

"Half the life of a policeman," Grijpstra said. "Hang around and wait."

"And another quarter goes to following the wrong track."

"We may be doing that right now."

"No," the commissaris said. "We are on the right track. But where's Sharif? He is so close I can feel him. Good evening, inspector."

The man the commissaris greeted was young—under thirty—a narrow-shouldered tall man with short blond hair and a thick beard and mustache that grew into each other. A very energetic man who couldn't keep still and kept waving his long arms about.

The commissaris began explaining the case to him.

"A glider pilot," the inspector said, "yes, yes. We have a small airport close by and there are gliders there. Is there anything else you know about him?"

"Nothing, except that he is a crack shot."

"That's something," the inspector said. "There's a shooting club here as well. I haven't been in Middelburg long. I was transferred six months ago from The Hague, but my colleague will know. I'll phone him."

The conversation took a long while but the inspector looked pleased when he put the phone down. "I think I can identify the man, sir, and I have a lot of details about him as well. His name is Heins, Jan Heins. He was born in Middelburg and has lived here most of his life. He must be nearly fifty years old. No police record. He served as a volunteer in the Korean War. Champion of the local shooting club."

"What does he do for a living?"

"He deals in antique furniture and arms. I know his shop. I am interested in antique arms myself and I have been in the shop but the prices are too high for me. He's got a lovely collection of dueling pistols."

"If he deals in antiques, he must do some traveling."

"Yes, sir; he is often away. His shop is closed when he isn't here."

"Does he have a gliding plane?"

"Yes, sir. When the weather is right he uses it almost every day."

"What's he like?"

"Very quiet, sir; never speaks unless he has to."

"We'll have to arrest him right now," the commissaris said, "he'll be asleep. Do you have some men to help us?"

"I'll have to phone them. There are only a few constables on duty now—only two, in a patrol car. The others are at home."

"Can you reach the men on duty?"

"Yes, sir, by radio."

"Right. Get hold of about four men to help us with the arrest and tell the men in the patrol car to drive about and hunt for a gray Jaguar. I have the registration number here. There are two Arabs in the car but they shouldn't interfere with them unless they have to. Tell them to be careful; I wouldn't be surprised if our friends were armed."

The inspector began to telephone and the desk sergeant spoke into the radio microphone on his desk. Within half an hour four uniformed constables had reported to the desk.

"Now," the commissaris said, "what about the house this Flyer lives in. Do you know where he sleeps?"

"My colleague told me, sir," the inspector said. "He's been into the house once. Jan Heins sleeps above his shop, second story. We can reach the window from the street with a ladder but it'll be awkward carrying a ladder around. I'll get our fire truck."

"Do you have any suggestions, inspector?"

The inspector scratched about in his short hair, pulled his beard and waved his arms about. "If he is the killer you think he is, he'll have a pistol near his bed. If we ring the bell it'll be in his hand. He'll probably have his bedroom window open but the opening won't be big enough to let a man in. Can't we wait until tomorrow, sir? I could dress up as a postman and pretend to deliver a telegram. Then I could pull a gun on him and he'd have to come quietly. Right now it'll be very tricky. We may have to jump through one of his bedroom windows."

"No," the commissaris said, "we can't wait. Sharif is close and *he* wants the Flyer as well. I don't know what Sharif plans to do. I think he suspects that we know who the killer is or may know any minute. That's why he raced out here. If we catch your Mr. Heins we catch Sharif as well, for Heins will talk. So Sharif has to get the killer out of the way. He may offer him money and tell him to disappear but it's more likely that he'll do away with him. And he is close, inspector. He is right here, I think, somewhere in your city."

"Yes, yes, yes, yes," the inspector said, furiously tearing at his beard. "But your Arab will kill in some devious way, not by breaking into Heins's house in the middle of the night. Maybe he intends to walk into his shop tomorrow and use a knife. I am sure Sharif doesn't expect you to be here already. You have done a very quick job."

"I think we should jump him," de Gier said. "You say his bedroom is on the second floor?"

"Yes. And he sleeps alone; he never married."

"We can drive your fire truck into the street; I'll be on it when it reaches the house. If you lend me gloves, something to protect my head and a thick coat, I'll jump right through the window. I'll have my pistol at his head before he wakes up. Meanwhile Grijpstra can force the door downstairs and rush up through the shop. The local constables should be in the garden or courtyard behind the house and in the street. It should be all over in a minute."

"Will that be all right, inspector?" the commissaris asked.

"Yes, sir," the inspector said. "The fire truck is outside. We can go if you're ready."

The fire truck was modern. Instead of a ladder, it had a giant metal cup connected to a long arm. De Gier and the inspector got into the cup, which had been raised to the proper height for the job. As the truck drove toward the house, the inspector guided the firemen below with arm signals. Grijpstra was waiting at the shop door. The commissaris' Citroën was parked opposite the next house and two of the local constables were posted in the street. The commissaris and his driver were waiting near the Citroën. The driver looked very worried.

"Now," the inspector whispered and de Gier crashed through the window that the inspector had pointed out to him. He kept his head down and the window glass spattered around the steel helmet he had borrowed from the desk sergeant. He had meant to roll over his head and land on his feet near the Flyer's bed but a small table covered with books obstructed his jump and he fell on his shoulder. His foot was stuck under a heavy lamp that fell with the table. The figure in the bed was up before de Gier could free himself and the Flyer's pistol was almost in position when the inspector came crashing in. The inspector was more fortunate. He landed on his feet and the impact of his jump carried him through to the other end of the room. The Flyer was knocked back onto his bed and his pistol fired but the bullet hit the floor. De Gier, finally free from table, books, lamp and cord, grabbed the Flyer's arm, twisted the pistol free and held his hands so that the inspector could handcuff him.

"There," de Gier said.

Grijpstra and the commissaris were also in the room by now.

"You're under arrest, Mr. Heins," the commissaris said.

The man in pajamas nodded.

"Commissaris!" came the sleepy-eyed constable's voice from the street.

The commissaris stuck his head through the broken window.

"You're wanted on the radio, sir, urgent. It's the sergeant from the station here."

The commissaris ran down the stairs.

"Yes?"

"Our car found the gray Jaguar, sir. At the airport. Two men were seen tinkering with Mr. Heins's glider on the field. My constables tried to arrest them but they got away. They're pursuing the car now and calling for assistance. I have alerted the State Police. My constables think that the suspects are heading back toward the Zeeland bridge. Over."

"Thank you, sergeant; we are going that way too. Your men will be bringing in Mr. Heins. Lock him up until we return. We'll be taking him to Amsterdam later today. Keep us informed about the Jaguar. Out."

The black Citroën shot away. The inspector was next to the constable at the wheel and the commissaris and de Gier were both holding on to Grijpstra, who sat in the middle of the back seat, leaning forward so that he could see where the car was going. The inspector was guiding the driver through the narrow streets of the city of Middelburg. Seemingly interminable rows of small gable houses were flashing past. Then a church, the magnificent complex of the city hall and an open streetmarket. "Siren," the commissaris shouted and a ghostly whine accompanied them. De Gier had shoved a blue flashing light onto the roof where it sat on a hook. They didn't want to hit the milkman or the baker's assistants who would be on their way to work by now. It was past six o'clock in the morning.

De Gier was still thinking of the pale face of the Flyer. He had looked reasonably calm, as if he had expected helmeted detectives to fly through his window in the middle of the night.

The radio came to life again. "He's on the bridge, sir," the sergeant's voice said. "I alerted the State Police and they have a car at the other side of the bridge but he doesn't know it. He can't see the car; the bridge is over seventeen kilometers long. My constables are blocking his rear. He'll never get away."

"How far are we from the bridge, inspector?" the commissaris asked.

"At this speed we'll be there in a few minutes, sir. Holy christ man, you're driving at a hundred ninety kilometers an hour."

"Yes, sir," the constable said. He had his foot flat down and the Citroën's engine was growling. The car could go a little faster still but he had had to break for a rather sharp curve. The Citroën didn't mind the curves. Its front-wheel drive made it bite into the tarred surface of the speedway every time the constable turned the wheel.

"The bridge," the inspector shouted, "slow down. The police car and the Jaguar will be very close." They saw the wreck a minute later. Sharif's driver had braked when he saw the blue flash on the State Police car ahead. He had probably had too much speed or he might have been too nervous to control the car, for it had hit the fence on the right, bounced back and hit the steel rail on the left. According to the State Police the car had bounced from right rail to left rail and back again like a marble in a pinball machine. When it finally stopped Sharif's body was already crushed.

The commissaris bent over the dying Arab. "Sharif," he said.

Sharif's eyes were open but there was no expression in them.

The commissaris looked up. The bridge was empty. The two police cars that blocked the bridge at each end and had turned it into a trap were so far away that they were hardly visible; only their blue flashing lights showed. Thick clouds filtered the early morning light and the infinite gray steel railing tapered off toward the horizon on both sides. All around them was the dark expanse of the sea, metallic in the ghostly light.

The Jaguar had squeezed itself into the railing, breaking through so that its nose stuck into space. Grijpstra, de Gier and the sleepy-eyed constable were huddled near the open doors of the Citroën. De Gier had a hand on the Arab driver's shoulder. The young Arab wasn't hurt at all. His eyes were on Sharif's body, and he was saying something.

"In the name of Allah," the young Arab said slowly, "the Compassionate, the Merciful."

About the Author

Born and raised in Amsterdam, Janwillem van de Wetering moved to South Africa when he was nineteen. After living and working there for six years he went to London where he studied philosophy for a year. From London he went to Kyoto, Japan, and lived in a Zen monastery for the next two years. His travels next took him to Peru and Colombia in South America where he got married and spent three years. From South America he went to Australia for a year and then returned to Amsterdam. He went into business and joined the Amsterdam Reserve Police Force where he swiftly rose through the ranks. Van de Wetering and his wife moved to Maine ten years ago and still make their home there.

His varied travels and police experience give van de Wetering's books a special quality. He is the author of THE EMPTY MIRROR, THE RATTLE-RAT, TUMBLEWEED, THE JAPANESE CORPSE, INSPECTOR SAITO'S SMALL SATORI, and MURDER BY REMOTE CONTROL, a mystery told in comic book format.